6/88

PIT BULL

ALSO BY SCOTT ELY

Starlight

PIT BULL

A Novel
Scott Ely

Weidenfeld & Nicolson
New York

Published by Weidenfeld & Nicolson, New York
A Division of Wheatland Corporation
10 East 53rd Street
New York, NY 10022

Published in Canada by General Publishing Company, Ltd.

The author gratefully acknowledges permission to reprint from the poem
"I have gone marking" from *Twenty Love Poems and a Song of Despair*,
by Pablo Neruda, translated by W. S. Merwin. English language translation
Copyright © 1969 by W. S. Merwin. All rights reserved. Reprinted by
permission of the Estate of Pablo Neruda, W. S. Merwin, Jonathan Cape Ltd.,
and Viking Penguin Inc.

Library of Congress Cataloging-in-Publication Data

Ely, Scott.
Pit bull.

I. Title.
PS3555.L94P58   1988   813′.54   87-37161
ISBN 1-55584-046-9

Manufactured in the United States of America

Designed by Irving Perkins Associates, Inc.

First Edition

10   9   8   7   6   5   4   3   2   1

For Cindy and Laura

PIT BULL

Chapter One

Jack Purse regarded his father Dexter's plan to get his land back by fighting the single pit bull left in his kennels as a sign the old man was losing his grip on things. No one was going to bet against a dog that always won. And all week Earl Blackmon, who was old but smart, had been pleading with Dexter that the way for all of them to hang on to their Delta land was to grow marijuana on an island in the Mississippi River. Jack hoped Dexter would continue to be stubborn so in the end the old man would end up working for him.

The pit bull at Jack's feet, a medium-sized black dog with yellow eyes, shook his head, rattling a swivel heavy enough to hold a bear, the swivel connecting the collar to the chain ending in a nylon strap that Jack kept wrapped around his wrist. Alligator had a dry, acrid stink that filled the pilothouse of the riverboat, a stink that never washed off, no matter how many times Jack swam him in the lake.

"Muzzle that dog," his father said from his seat in an armchair by the big mahogany wheel.

Dexter was big, bigger even than Jack, the fat of middle age thick on him, the muscles sagging in his chest, his face always covered with sweat now the weather had turned hot. He wore long-sleeved work shirts winter and summer, the top button always fastened, and a pair of high-top basketball shoes.

"Only job you got is caring for that dog. Can't even do that right," Dexter continued.

"I'll farm. I'll have my own place," Jack said.

"Go to the Greenville bank and try to borrow the money," he said. "Won't give you a dime. Try the insurance company that owns Grandfather Purse's land."

"You'll see. I'll have my place," Jack said. "Blackmon's got a way."

The old man snorted in disgust and said, "Earl's a damn fool."

"He's thought it all out. It'll work."

"We got a share in this boat. And the island."

The riverboat was moored to the shore of the oxbow lake created when the Corps of Engineers straightened a loop in the river by cutting a new channel, the lake still connected to the river at the south end, the old riverbank now a long crescent-shaped island. Dexter and his friends used the boat as a clubhouse and hunted deer on the island.

"Most important, we got Alligator," Dexter said. "Forget about Blackmon."

"Nobody'll bet with you," Jack said. "Won't get a single fight."

"You let me worry about that," Dexter said.

Jack looked across the lake to the big island's green wall of trees, willows growing thick on the shoreline and inland fuzzy-topped cypresses rising above the oaks and hickories.

"Had to listen to Earl Blackmon talk about growing that shit all week," Dexter said. "Now he's bringing the whole courthouse out to convince them. Sheriff, mayor, prosecuting attorney."

"I'm going in with Blackmon," Jack said. "Buy back the land with my share."

"Then you're as big a fool as Earl."

"I didn't lose our land."

"My land," Dexter said. "You remember that. Land's been in our family a hundred and fifty years."

"Well, it ain't in the family now. You lost it all by yourself. Never asked me how to run things."

"You getting smart with me?" Dexter asked, talking slow the way he always did when he was mad.

Keep cool, Jack thought.

"No, sir," Jack said.

Dexter said, "Together we could get it back. Dog'll fight for you."

"I won't be working your corner," Jack said.

Dexter gave a heavy sigh and started to get up. Jack got ready for a fight.

Then Dexter settled back and said, "You'll remember who you are when the time comes."

"Not likely," Jack said.

Jack liked seeing the old man sweat but wondered what he was doing there watching. Maybe it was because it was so good to see the old man down. Except for the army and one year at Mississippi State, he had worked for no one but the old man since high school, waiting for the land to become his.

Dexter said, "Boy, are you going to muzzle that dog?"

"He won't bite me," Jack said, and petted the top of the dog's head.

Alligator looked up. Jack was never sure about him. He always carried a wedge-shaped breaking stick, whittled from a piece of Grandfather Purse's hickory cane, in his belt just in case the dog latched on to someone and he had to pry his jaws loose. Yet he let the dog sleep in his room on a rug beside his bed. He liked having control over his father's prize animal.

"I ain't worried about you," Dexter said. "My neighbors and yours will be here soon. He bites one of them, there'll be a lawsuit. You put the muzzle on him."

Jack thought about not doing it, telling the old man to go to hell. But instead he put the muzzle on Alligator, who endured as always in silence.

"Can you talk to that dog?" Dexter asked. "The niggers say you can." Dexter laughed and continued, "Goddamn insurance company. I'm an endangered species. Like that dog. People up in Washington want to outlaw me. Just because I want to be a free man."

Jack stroked Alligator's head, the coat smooth beneath his fingertips. No puncture scars or ragged ears.

Alligator's ears stood up, and the dog looked toward the open door of the pilothouse. But he did not bark. Jack seldom heard Alligator make a sound.

Blackmon walked into the cabin but stopped when he saw Alligator. He looked the picture of a gentleman farmer: polished boots and a seersucker suit with a blue tie. He carried a book with a green cover under his arm.

"Don't worry, we got the muzzle on him," Dexter said.

"Then you're smart," Blackmon said. "That's a crazy dog. What comes of breeding fathers to daughters. Got a strong bite and good moves but no gameness."

"He's dead game," Dexter said, the words coming out of his mouth so slow Alligator raised his head.

"Hell, Dexter, you don't know that," Blackmon said.

Jack knew the only way to find out if Alligator was dead game was to fight him to the death and see if he held on even after he was dead.

Dexter said, "You got the dog that'll beat him?"

Blackmon and Dexter had been rivals in dogfighting for years. But Dexter would have to be careful about the fight. The TV station in Memphis had done a report on dogfighting, and the result had been that a convention in Tupelo was infiltrated by an undercover state trooper. People were fined. The real loss was the destruction of valuable dogs by the state as dangerous animals. Now there was talk of banning the breed.

"Would if you let your boy work my corner," Blackmon said.

"He don't like to work in the pit," Dexter said. "Pretty, though. Women like him just fine." He grinned at Jack and said, spitting the words out as he would a stream of tobacco juice, "Pretty boy."

"Don't be so hard on the boy," Blackmon said. "He went to Vietnam. Got wounded."

Jack had caught the enemy frag on the hop, stretching to get his hands on it as if it were a slow short throw to first base, but a burst of rifle fire caused him to put his head down for a moment before he threw it back. The frag went off only a few meters away. He was lucky to escape with only shrapnel in his arm and chest. The scars remained, raised white welts snaking across his chest. Dexter was proud of his Bronze Star.

"I'll take Alligator back to the truck," Jack said.

"Stay right there," Dexter said. And then to Blackmon, "See, I can't even get him mad. We used to have some good fights. Could always put him on the ground. Still can."

Am I waiting for him to get old and sick? Jack thought. So I can be sure I can take him?

The others showed up. First Wade dressed in his khaki sheriff's uniform and then the mayor along with Norris, the district attorney, in lawyer's pinstripe. Evelyn, the mayor, always wore a tailored suit and high heels. They were the officials of nothing because Egypt Ridge, although still the county seat, had long ago been reduced to a courthouse, a jail, and one store. A dozen families, black and white, still lived there.

"Jack, I drove by your mother's park yesterday," Evelyn said. "Next real high water we get, it'll be gone."

The old man had made a park for his mother beside the river, ripped out the cane and briars and planted fescue. He built an arbor with seats made of cypress boards from an old barn, and a fishpond.

Jack wished he had the frag in his hand so he could toss it to the old man. That would be a sweet way to watch him die. His mother had gotten tired of the women in Memphis and the young girl in New Orleans and the one everyone said he kept in Greenwood, and she had left. She traveled on her family's money, sending Jack gifts from all over the world. One year at Christmas he would receive a machete from Brazil and the next a music box from Switzerland. She refused to return to the Delta, despite the letters he wrote asking her to come. It was as if from his father's blood he had received some sort of terrible disease that chilled even a mother's love.

"Go ahead and talk, Earl," Dexter said. "You can start wasting their time like you been doing mine."

"Least I still got my land," Blackmon said. "I plan to keep it."

"You boys hush up," Evelyn said. "Let's hear what Earl's got to say."

Dexter took a shotgun off a rack and began to take it apart, laying each part out carefully on a cloth.

"All of us have failed at farming," Blackmon said. "I still got my land. If I don't have a good year, I'll go under too. Goddamn insurance company'll end up with it. Norris lost his daddy's place last spring. That nice thousand acres Evelyn got from her uncle is gone. We can't make a living hauling tourists up and down the river on this boat."

Thirty years before they had brought the boat up from New Orleans and through the channel into the lake.

Blackmon held the green book above his head.

"This'll get us back our land," Blackmon said.

"Earl, are you drunk?" Evelyn asked.

Blackmon laughed and said, "Hell, no. I was the one thought up making you mayor, Evelyn. They loved you in Washington. Only female mayor in Mississippi. Got us some money because of that."

"He's drunk," Norris said.

Wade said, "Be quiet. Let Earl talk."

"This book tells you how to grow marijuana," Blackmon said. "Put the big field on Bear Island in plants, and we'll all buy our land back."

"We'll get caught," Norris said.

"No, this is the first time a whole county government's been in on it," Blackmon said.

"Earl's right," Evelyn said.

"We'll grow a special kind called sinsemilla. We can get about a million-five a ton for it wholesale, maybe more. I figure we can put at least ten thousand plants on the island," Blackmon said, holding up the book again.

"We don't know anything about growing marijuana," Norris said.

Alligator shook his head, rattling the swivel. Everyone was quiet while Jack petted him.

Blackmon said, "If we grow it right, we'll get a yield of about two pounds per plant."

Jack wondered what Dexter was going to say, but the old man remained bent over the shotgun, poking at it with a screwdriver. Jack's scars itched and he scratched them, knowing that irritated Dexter.

"That's fifteen million dollars!" Norris said.

Everyone began to talk at the same time. Blackmon raised his hands for silence.

"We're good farmers. We can grow anything," Blackmon said. "Last year I set a record for production. Couldn't sell my beans for enough to cover expenses."

Jack knew what had happened, could recite it by heart from listening to Dexter complain. First there had been the Nixon embargo on soybeans. Then the Brazilian government and others started to subsidize bean production. Fuel prices went up. Bean and cotton prices went down. They tried winter wheat, sunflowers. Nothing made money, no matter how efficiently they grew it.

Wade got up and took the book from Blackmon. He sat down by Jack and started flipping through it. The title was *Marijuana Growing Made Easy.*

Jack wanted Blackmon to convince them. He wanted to buy land just like the rest of them, five hundred acres. Later he would have a house and a wife and children. They had lost their land, but he had not even had a chance to own his yet. He liked the way things were developing. The old man was sitting on the sidelines, nobody paying any attention to him.

"What about pirates sneaking in to steal the crop?" Wade asked.

Norris said, "You going to let the members of the club in on this?"

"The town?" Evelyn asked.

Blackmon laughed and raised his hands for silence.

"We'll let everybody in," Blackmon said. "Everybody'll get shares." He paused and continued, "Some bigger ones than others."

They all laughed.

Jack listened to them talk, arguing about how much money they were going to make. Norris was afraid of getting caught and Evelyn and Wade tried to reassure him. Alligator got up and lay down. Everyone was still while he did it.

"I've got a wife and kids," Norris kept saying.

Finally Blackmon made them shut up.

"It's up to you to convince the rest of the town," Blackmon said. "Unless everybody agrees, there's no use doing it."

"He's right," Wade said. "Most people get caught because their neighbors turn them in."

"What about the niggers?" Norris asked.

"Them too," Blackmon said. "Everybody."

"The preacher?" Evelyn said.

"Especially him," Blackmon said. "Bascomb's been trying to raise money for a new church. Says he wants to leave something behind for folks to remember him by."

Then Blackmon turned to the old man and said, "Dexter, you going to stand by your neighbors?"

"High water?" Dexter said. "That island's more water than dirt."

"You've been renting a field out there to Tom Cochran," Blackmon said.

"Yeah, and he loses his crop of beans every couple of years," Dexter said. "Remember, we let him grow crops mainly for the deer and ducks."

"Dexter's right—," Norris began.

"Shut up," Blackmon said.

"I won't have anything to do with it," Dexter said.

"What about you, Jack?" Blackmon asked.

"I'm in," Jack said, wondering what it was going to feel like to get the edge on the old man.

Blackmon said, "Dexter, Tom's renting your land. It don't say in the contract what he grows. Tom's with us."

"That's up to Tom," Dexter said. He looked hard at Blackmon with the beginnings of a smile on his face. "You considered growing those plants might be harder than you think?"

"It's worth the risk," Evelyn said. "I can hardly make payments on my house. I'm not going to end up in an apartment in Greenville."

"I got children to send to college," Norris said.

Dexter shrugged his shoulders and said, "I see your minds are made up."

"You can come in with us any time," Blackmon said. "Just say the word."

"I'm down. Why should I want to get kicked?" Dexter said.

He began to reassemble the gun.

They left and for a while Jack and Dexter sat in silence, Jack stroking Alligator's head.

"You remember when we'd wrestle after you got too big to whip?" Dexter asked.

Jack said nothing.

"Answer me," Dexter continued. "You ain't wearing a muzzle."

"I do," Jack said.

"We were close then," Dexter said. "Father and son."

"Then Mama left."

"Boy, you're a grown man, and you ain't learned a damn thing about women."

Jack got up off the bench and unwrapped the strap from around his wrist.

"You made her leave!" Jack said.

"Haven't noticed Margaret coming back to see you," Dexter said. "Or ask you to visit her. Guess she's too busy."

"It's because I'm your goddamn son."

"No son of mine would be so damn stupid."

"You cared more about your dogs than her."

"You stayed around here and worked on the place. Waiting for my land. Waiting for me to die. Now you let them take you in with that fool scheme. You'll like chopping cotton at Parchman."

"Least I'm not like you. You're the one who always says a man's got to be hard to survive."

Dexter laughed.

"Hard, not stupid. You better be studying about being like me if you plan to throw in with Blackmon," Dexter said. Then he continued, "Take that dog on home. I've got work to do."

Jack left the cabin. At his truck he took the muzzle off Alligator. He had learned to watch the dog's moods carefully. Sometimes he could tell just by the way Alligator carried his tail that it was safer to keep the muzzle on him. It was when his eyes glazed over, a smoky white film over the gold, that he became dangerous. The dog had never tried to bite him, but Jack knew he would give no warning when that day came.

He drove his truck away from the boat, the tires bouncing in the ruts, raising twin plumes of dust. He crossed the levee and went past the row of catfishermen's shacks. A little man with a beard, cleaning a shotgun on the hood of a truck, stared but did not wave. Now the land was perfectly flat, scored by geometrical rows of cotton and soybeans, all belonging to owners who lived far away from the Delta.

Jack stroked Alligator, looking into those yellow eyes that never looked away, and smelled his stink. He wished he was more like the dog, indifferent to anything the old man did, content to eat and sleep and wait for his chance to grab hold and not let go.

Chapter Two

Jack saw the vet's blue truck pull into the yard. He walked off the porch and followed the truck around to the back. The house, built with an enclosed breezeway down the center and rooms on each side, the kitchen in the back, was on five acres of land they still owned, house and yard free and clear of debt. Out back the gravel driveway ran under a sign: TOP DOG KENNELS: HOME OF FIGHTERS THAT FIGHT AND WIN, OR DIE TRYING.

That's the old man, Jack thought. Charging through life with a big hard-on. Wants me to become like him, like Alligator. Mean and crazy.

"Come give me and Squirrel a hand," Dexter said as the vet got out of his truck.

Jack did not know whether Dexter called his friend Davenport Lee Shipp "Squirrel" because of his protruding front teeth or whether it was because Davenport always won the squirrel-hunting contest they held on opening day each year. The woods crawled with snakes, but the old man and Squirrel watched the treetops instead of the ground. The first time Jack went with them he watched the ground and returned with three cottonmouths and a canebrake rattler, but no squirrels. They laughed and laughed and gave him the game to clean.

Dogs no longer ran back and forth on chains attached by pulleys to hundred-foot cables, the pulleys whirring on the wires. Dexter believed letting the dogs run the cables gave them more exercise than pacing about a pen. Some dogs used to be kept on short chains attached to car axles sunk in the ground, waiting their turn on the

13

cables. No dogs sat in the shade of the shelters built at each end of the cable runs. No dogs ran the treadmills Dexter used for conditioning. The catmill with its long weighted arm and cage, in which Dexter kept a Halloween mask of a goblin as a lure instead of a cat, was empty. The gates to the runs for pregnant bitches stood open. Dexter had sold off his dogs, fifty in all, to raise cash and avoid feed bills. Only Alligator sat beneath the shade of his shelter.

"What's going on?" Jack asked.

"I told you I'd get my land back," Dexter said. "Alligator'll do it for me."

"Good luck on getting a fight," Jack said.

Alligator had been fought just twice. The second fight had happened because nobody had believed the first, Alligator boring in under his opponent, then lifting and flipping the bewildered dog before the astonished crowd and catching him with those steel-trap jaws midway along the backbone, severing the spine with one bite. They had to see it again, thought what they had witnessed must surely have been some magic trick. So they held another match and sacrificed a good dog to Alligator because watching him do it to a cur would have proved nothing.

"Earl thinks that Texas Firecracker dog of his can beat Alligator," Dexter said. "Firecracker dog outweighs him by twenty pounds. Earl thinks he has the advantage." Then he turned to Jack and continued, "With you in the pit we'd win for sure."

"I won't do it," Jack said.

"Leave the boy alone," Squirrel said.

"That land bought the clothes on his back," Dexter said, talking slow. "Now he won't help get it back."

"With Alligator it won't matter who's in the pit," Squirrel said.

Jack had been to his first and only dogfight when he was twelve. Blackmon and the old man had matched their dogs at a convention in Ruleville. Dexter matched a little bitch called High Cotton against Blackmon's best dog, bragging all the time to the crowd that she would fight well because his boy, who had a way with dogs, was in the pit.

Jack remembered how High Cotton had felt under his hands as he held her in their corner, waiting her turn to scratch, her body quivering with anticipation. She was too much dog for a boy to handle, but he held on out of fear of the old man. And then at the referee's signal, he released her; she barely touched the ground as she ran straight across the pit at the dog held in its corner by Blackmon. Jack knew that under his touch she wanted to fight, to please him. It was more than her just being a game dog.

High Cotton died in Jack's arms in the back seat of the car on their way home.

Dexter continued, "But the real money'll come in stud fees."

"Alligator kills bitches," Jack said. "Putting a muzzle on him don't do any good. He's only interested in fighting."

"That's why Squirrel is here," Dexter said. "We'll collect Alligator's juice. After the fight, every breeder in the country'll want some of it."

Jack helped them unload the equipment: a self-contained liquid-nitrogen refrigerator, milk as a semen extender, an artificial vagina, and plastic straws for storage. The AV had hollow walls filled with hot water to protect the semen from the shock of cold air and a collection tube at one end. The vet had brought along a hound bitch in heat to stimulate Alligator.

Squirrel had always helped Dexter care for his dogs injured in the pit. He saved many of Dexter's dogs when other handlers would have been forced to put a bullet through their heads. The vet had trained Dexter to be a better-than-average veterinary surgeon.

"He'll try to kill the bitch," Jack said.

"Maybe, but the doc has something that'll take care of Mr. Alligator," Dexter said.

The vet pulled out a metal rod that looked to Jack like a cattle prod, only much shorter.

"We'll use this to electrically stimulate his vesicular glands once the bitch has gotten him excited," Squirrel said as he began to coat the rod with Vaseline. "The finest electroejaculator on the market."

Squirrel loved scientific equipment. Dexter claimed the vet had the best-equipped surgery in the South.

"You want me to put the muzzle on him?" Jack asked.

"No, I'll take care of that," Dexter said.

Jack sat on the back steps and watched Dexter muzzle Alligator. Then they brought the bitch out of the truck. It took both of them to bring Alligator close enough to sniff her. And after they got him there, he lunged at her head, sending the bitch howling.

"Maybe she's not good-looking enough," Jack said.

Dexter glared at him but said nothing.

"Forget the bitch," Squirrel said. "The ejaculator'll take care of him."

"Jack, come here and hold the collection tube," Dexter said.

Jack exposed the penis and using tape and sterile gauze secured it to the collection tube. Alligator smelled like the bottom of the lake at low water after it had baked dry in the sun, littered with bits of dried weed, mussel shells, and gar heads. Then the vet slid the ejaculator up Alligator's anus. Alligator did not tremble or complain but was oblivious to the whole procedure.

"Get ready," Squirrel said, as he turned a dial set in the handle of the ejaculator.

For a moment Alligator was still. Then his whole body began to tremble. But nothing was flowing into the tube.

"Watch out!" Dexter shouted. "Hold him!"

Alligator lunged, Jack falling backwards, seeing the dog and the men frozen for an instant before the men fell away and the dog ran free, the tube still taped to his penis. The tube fell off as he headed straight for the bitch. Squirrel sat on the ground holding the ejaculator, the probe glistening in the sunlight. Alligator had run right over Dexter, his claws leaving scratches on the old man's face.

The bitch tried to hide under the truck, but her chain was too short. Alligator bowled her over and despite the muzzle started looking for a hold. Jack could see his jaws working, teeth flashing in the sunlight. Before they could reach them, the bitch broke her chain, but Alligator pinned her against the wheel. When she tried to grab his leg, he knocked her down with one paw, the blow delivered like a roundhouse right from a boxer, sending her howling in the dust. She ran across the yard, Alligator close behind, until her chain caught under the edge of a treadmill. Alligator rubbed his nose in the dirt, trying to rid himself of the muzzle. Failing, he went for a chest hold on the bitch, who howled in terror at Alligator's jaws clicking so close to where she lived.

It took all three of them to get Alligator off the bitch.

"Goddamn dog ain't of this world," Dexter said. "Wasn't whelped. Crawled right up out of hell."

Jack remembered when Alligator was whelped to the bitch Sugar Candy. They knew from the first Alligator was going to be special. As a puppy out on the cable run, he learned to kill chickens. By pretending to be asleep, he lured them within range, killing them with one swift, sure bite to the head. Then in his first training roll against an experienced but toothless dog, he had killed his opponent before Dexter could stop him.

"We'll have Jack stimulate him while we hold his nose to the bitch," Squirrel said.

"What d'you mean?" Jack asked.

Dexter laughed.

"Why, give that dog a handjob," Dexter said. "He likes you."

"I'm not doing that," Jack said.

Dexter said, "Boy, it's just a dumb animal. Nobody'll ever accuse you of liking anything but women. Army had me do the same thing for my guard dog. Was a standing order. Did it once a week. Damn dog loved me for it."

"No way," Jack said.

"Do like you're told," Dexter said, talking slow and making Alligator's ears stand up.

"We'll bring him up close to the bitch again," Squirrel said.

"He's not interested," Jack said.

"It can't hurt," Dexter said. "Maybe he'll discover there's something in his life besides killing."

They brought Alligator's nose up to the whimpering bitch.

"You do it," Jack said to Dexter.

"That dog hates me," Dexter said. "You're the only one he likes. We sell enough Gator juice and we're on our way to getting our land back."

"You said it was yours, not mine," Jack said.

"You're making me mad," Dexter said.

"Okay," Jack said. "But I don't want to hear about this next time I go to Greenville."

Dexter said, "Nobody'd think it was worth telling but you."

The two men struggled to hold Alligator. The dog did not kick or twist about, just moved steadily one way and then another to test the men's strength. Jack knelt beside the dog, smelling Alligator's stink.

"Go ahead," Squirrel said.

Jack massaged Alligator's penis, feeling the dog's heat. Alligator became excited, swelling to fill the AV as Jack guided him into it. Alligator trembled. The bitch began to howl.

"How long?" Jack asked.

Squirrel said, "For dogs it takes a long time."

"He don't have a drop in him," Jack said. "We're wasting our time."

"Don't you stop," Dexter said.

Jack wondered why he was doing it and not the old man. Suddenly Alligator began to come in short spurts, the milky-white semen trickling into the collection bottle at the bottom of the AV. Jack smelled the sour scent of it, all mixed up with the stink of the dog. Then the smell of the last woman he had been with, a girl in a motel in Memphis, appeared out of nowhere, and he stopped.

"Don't stop now," Squirrel said. "You're doing beautiful. Dogs go a long time."

Jack put his hand back on the dog, and Alligator began to come again.

"We'll be able to make a thousand Alligators," Dexter said.

"Not that many," Squirrel said. "Maybe we can inseminate ten bitches with what we've collected today."

"This boy is so good at it we can do it once a week at least," Dexter said. "Took this long to find out what he does best."

"You'll never make enough money off this," Jack said. "We won't even be able to pay the taxes on the house."

"You let me worry about that," Dexter said. "Keep working that dog."

Alligator continued to fill the collection bottle for what seemed to Jack like five minutes.

Then it was over. They put Alligator back on the cable while Jack went to wash his hands with the hose.

Squirrel checked the sperm content of a sample with a photometer and pronounced it excellent.

"This machine cost me plenty," Squirrel said. "But it's a lot easier than making a count with a microscope."

Then they mixed the semen with the milk and cooled the mixture down to five degrees centigrade. Five hours later they added glycerol to protect the sperm from freezing and placed samples in clear plastic straws that they sealed and stored under liquid nitrogen in the refrigerator.

It was late afternoon. Alligator slept in the shade of his plywood shelter. The sun came through the big windows of the porch, which Jack's mother once kept filled with plants. Now the glass shelves were empty. The squat stainless-steel refrigerator, which looked like a miniature space capsule, sat on a table surrounded by empty clay flowerpots.

Jack held a straw up to the light. Milk crystals sparkled in the sunlight, Alligator's sap locked in the ice, awaiting life at the pleasure of the old man. Jack shuddered at the thought of fierce dogs whose only love was battle, matched in a thousand pits.

Chapter Three

Jack helped them grade the marijuana on the riverboat. Blackmon and Wade had flown down to Mexico in Blackmon's plane to pick up seeds and samples of grass. Now they were testing the various samples for potency by smoking them and gauging the quality of the high. Only seeds from the best grass would be planted. None of Dexter's friends except Wade had gotten high before. Wade had done it as part of a course given by the Mississippi Narcotics Bureau to train local lawmen in drug enforcement.

The testing had been going on for a week, and they were down to the last few samples laid out on a long table in labeled plastic bags. The town was now in on the project, everyone assigned a share, even the children. Letting the children in on it had been Evelyn's idea.

"Come on and help," Blackmon said to Dexter. "This stuff is better than whiskey."

Dexter was drinking whiskey out of a coffee cup.

"No, thanks," Dexter said. "You boys've stunk up the whole boat."

"What about you?" Blackmon asked Evelyn.

Evelyn shook her head and said, "Once when Trey took me to Cuba to fish we tried cocaine. I liked that. Haven't tried it since."

Jack supposed that once she had been a beautiful woman. Now there were wrinkles around her eyes, her skin loose over the bones. Her husband, Trey, had fallen out of a boat on the way to a duck blind and drowned before they had a chance to have any children. As a boy Jack remembered seeing her supervising the bringing of her cotton to the gin. Then she had worn men's work clothes, and he already thought of her as an old lady.

He took a deep drag off a cigar-shaped joint and held the smoke in his lungs. When he blew it out, Alligator sneezed. Dexter was gradually filling the refrigerator with the dog's semen. Alligator had gotten used to the collections, and had quit attacking the bitch. But Jack hated collection day, listening to Squirrel and Dexter make jokes while he worked on Alligator.

Dexter said, "Take that dog outside."

"I'll do it," Norris said, staggering over to take hold of the chain.

Norris wore his striped tie around his head.

"You want to walk the hound of hell?" Jack asked.

They all laughed.

"Sure do," Norris said. Then he turned to Evelyn. "I'd like to have a pretty woman walk with me."

Evelyn said, "I remember when I used to help your mama change your diapers."

"Miss Evelyn is too much of a woman for you, sonny," Dexter said.

Norris started to say something but changed his mind.

That's right, Jack thought. Push little Norris around. It's easy.

Evelyn blushed and said, "Hush, Dexter."

Dexter paid attention and shut up.

Alligator's golden eyes shimmered, and Jack thought he knew what the dog was thinking as they said he could. He could feel the cypress boards beneath his bare feet even as Alligator could feel them with his belly. Could feel the power in those jaws. Knew what it was like to close them around an enemy, feeling the joy of battle fill his body so that for a moment he slipped away from the boat and was in the pit living free. It was like swinging out on the rope at the lake, that instant when he let go of the rope and paused, weightless, before falling to the water.

Norris tugged on the lead but Alligator remained on the floor, not even lifting his head.

"Go on, dog," Jack said.

He knew he should keep Norris from fooling with the dog. But suddenly he was afraid of Alligator, more afraid than he had been of long operations in the bad bush when they kept getting mortared and never saw the enemy. And he remembered lying on the ground, hoping if he got hit it would be by a round impacting on his head so he would be spared the pain of the shrapnel.

Alligator got up and followed Norris out onto the deck.

"Don't let him eat you," Dexter called after him.

They all laughed.

Blackmon and Wade agreed this last batch was the most powerful.

"The smoke tastes sweet. Like blended pipe tobacco," Blackmon said.

Blackmon and Wade left. They planned to return in the morning to begin germination tests on the seeds.

Dexter said, "Get Alligator back in here before Norris scares him to death."

Jack found them at the stern by the rail. Norris was kneeling in front of the dog, reminding Jack of pictures in Sunday school of pagans worshiping idols. Then Norris filled his lungs with smoke and blew a bluish cloud of it into Alligator's face.

"Get high, you fucking dog," Norris said.

Alligator sneezed once and then with one quick twist of his head bit a piece out of the end of Norris's ring finger, leaving the nail intact. He held it in his mouth for a moment before spitting it out onto the deck, the flesh covered with blood and foam.

Norris giggled and picked up the piece, trying to fit it back on his finger. Jack looked into Alligator's golden eyes.

"Why didn't you eat it, you bastard?" Jack said.

"Help me!" Norris screamed.

Alligator laid his ears back and trotted toward the other end of the boat, the chain rattling against the deck.

Jack made Norris hold his tie over the stump to try to stop the bleeding. Then he picked up the tip and took Norris inside, where Evelyn wrapped it in plastic wrap and put it in a cup of ice.

Blackmon picked up the cup, and the rest gathered around to look as if Evelyn had captured in it some strange creature from the lake. Norris sat on a bench cursing Alligator, whose chain was wrapped around a table leg.

"Don't you men stand around gawking," said Evelyn. "Let's get him to the hospital quick."

"I'll kill that dog," Norris kept saying over and over.

Finally Dexter got mad and said, "No, you won't. Stay away from Mr. Alligator. Or next time he'll bite your damn head off."

Norris shut up and began to cry.

At the Greenville hospital the doctor sewed the piece back on, assuring Norris it could easily be saved. Norris's wife, Sally Ann, showed up. She was mad at all of them, but especially at Dexter. Norris had been talking about a lawsuit and wanted Alligator destroyed. Then Dexter whispered to her that by conspiring to grow marijuana, Norris was already in a lot more trouble than getting chewed up.

"I told Norris a hundred times he should've taken a job in Jackson," Sally Ann said.

Jack knew Sally Ann was not about to start crying. And since she was not having much luck giving Dexter a hard time, then Norris was going to catch it from her when they got home.

When they left the hospital, it was dark. They rode the levee looking for deer, drinking from a bottle of whiskey. Jack rode with Alligator in the back of the truck. They passed the bottle through the window to him.

Deer were caught by the headlights, frozen in the glare, their eyes glowing red. Then they ran, white tails flashing as they bounded off the levee toward the trees.

"They're like smoke," Evelyn said. "Beautiful smoke."

"Pests," Dexter said. "Can eat up a field of beans."

"Daddy's not a sentimental man," Jack said.

"Boy doesn't know much about me," Dexter said. "Why, if Sally Ann had started crying, I might not've been so hard on her. Never could stand to see a pretty woman cry."

Evelyn laughed and said, "Dexter, you always were just a plain fool for a pretty woman. Been making 'em cry as long as I can remember."

"But not you?" Dexter asked.

"I'm too old for crying over men," Evelyn said.

"We're both getting old," Dexter said.

Then he leaned over and whispered something to her. She laughed and moved closer to him.

Jack wanted to tell Evelyn that Dexter had made Margaret cry plenty of times but said nothing. He finished the rest of the whiskey and threw the bottle toward the river, listening to the open end going whup, whup, whup as it went spinning away into the night.

At the house Dexter and Evelyn went in the kitchen to cook while Jack took Alligator back into his bedroom. He lay on the bed and tried to sleep, smelling the stink of the dog. He still had trouble sleeping, slipping back into the middle of a bad night ambush if he was not careful. For a time he had kept a shotgun under his bed. But one night Dexter had found him still half-asleep, wandering about the room with the gun locked and loaded, screaming for gunners to put up illumination. Dexter made him return the gun to the rack in the hall. But now he kept an Airlight .38 under his pillow. He liked to drift off to sleep with his hand on it.

Then the stink of the dog was replaced by the smell of catfish cooking. Evelyn and Dexter were frying it. He could hear them laughing from the kitchen.

Acting like fools, he thought.

Alligator had gone to sleep and growled from some pit dream he was having.

More than once he had thought of shooting Alligator and

destroying the frozen semen. That would end everything. But it was too easy that way. He wanted to see Dexter embarrassed before his friends. And Dexter might actually make his crazy scheme work and get the land back, land that could become his one day.

Evelyn called him to come eat. The effects of the marijuana were gone but he was feeling the whiskey. He felt like throwing up but knew Dexter would make fun of him if he did not eat.

"You don't look so good," Dexter said.

Jack sat down at the table.

"Evelyn made some hush puppies and slaw," Dexter continued. "I fried the fish."

Evelyn passed him the basket of hush puppies.

Jack bit into one of them.

"Not a bit greasy, is it?" Dexter said.

He wished Dexter would shut up. He had never shared the old man's enthusiasm for eating. Dexter ate raw liver, ripped steaming from the bucks he shot. He liked to make exotic dishes like snapping turtle stew served in the shell.

Jack ate a piece of catfish.

"How is it?" Dexter asked.

"Leave him alone and let him eat," Evelyn said.

"I put in plenty of black pepper along with a little beer in the batter," Dexter said.

The fish was excellent but Jack resisted telling Dexter. Eating made Jack feel better.

"Eats like he likes it," Dexter said.

Jack said nothing, thinking that Dexter had always been a good cook. Even when they had employed Ophelia, a black cook, Dexter had been the one who planned many of the meals and directed her in the kitchen, not his mother.

Dexter continued, "Me and Evelyn are going out to the Indian mound. She thinks there's three of her kin buried there. It was back during the big flood. Died of cholera. Had to be buried quick because it was hot and that was the only dry ground."

"If we find them, we'll have markers put up," Evelyn said.

Two fools lost in the past, Jack thought.

Both spent more time in the county graveyards than the preachers. Evelyn paid to have rubbings taken of her ancestors' stones, the first whites in the county, and had the stones incised because the lettering set in relief had been worn away by the elements.

Jack helped Evelyn clear the table while Dexter assembled lanterns, a shovel, and a metal detector.

"They buried 'em with at least a belt buckle," Dexter said, holding up the metal detector.

They left, walking between the rows of young cotton plants, which began at the edge of the yard. Jack sat on the back porch with Alligator and waited until the lanterns came on. Dexter kept the Indian mound grass cut, or they would have been confronted with an impassable tangle of brush. He had built benches there, and he was fond of going out to the mound at night to drink under the stars. Then the first lantern went out, followed by the second.

Alligator was jumping up and grabbing hold of the porch roof rafters and hanging on, a game he liked to play. The first time he did it Jack could not believe the dog could jump so high. He listened to the wood fibers creak as the dog tightened his hold. Then Alligator opened his jaws and dropped lightly to the ground.

Jack put Alligator on the cable and walked into the cotton. The old man had probably turned the lanterns off to look at the stars, and they could easily use the metal detector in the dark. He walked slowly, as if he were hunting or on patrol in the jungle, feeling the soft, tilled earth give under his feet. He had never had any fear of the dark, welcomed it when it came in the jungle, because he believed it gave him an edge over the enemy.

He heard them before he could see anything except the mound, a black hump rising out of the field. All the stars were out but there was no moon. Then he recognized the sounds of love, the suck of her on the old man's cock and his panting.

Jack began to crawl as he had done so many times in Vietnam, feeling ahead with his fingers to find the contours of the earth. This time he searched for twigs he might break instead of trip wires. If the cotton was high, it would have been easy, but now there was no cover. He could smell the plants and the fertilizer and a trace of last year's defoliant. Ahead the dark black mass of the mound looked as high as a mountain.

When he reached it, he crawled up the side of the mound, taking almost ten minutes by the luminescent dial of his watch. The mosquitoes were bad and he had to resist the impulse to slap at them. Instead he simply let them fill themselves with his blood and drop off.

They finished just as he reached the top, first Evelyn, giving a sharp cry like the call of a night bird, and then Dexter, groaning.

"Don't the skeeters bother you?" the old man asked.

She laughed.

"No, I'm too tough," she said.

Then the old man started quoting poetry at her, his voice heavy and rich in the dark.

"I have gone marking the atlas of your body with crosses of fire."

Jack supposed he would not have been more surprised if the old man had burst into flame and ascended into the night sky.

"Where did you learn that?" she asked.

"From a drunken lawyer in a bar in Caracas," Dexter said. "We were down there trying to find markets for soybeans."

"Say me some more," she said.

"That's all I know," he said. "He quoted it at us all night. First in Spanish and then in English. That one saying is all I remember."

"Again," she said.

And he did, this time speaking slower than the first.

"I'm not sure what it means," he said.

She said, "It doesn't matter."

They went at it again.

Jack listened to her or the old man slapping at mosquitoes. They giggled like a couple of kids balling on the levee. Jack felt himself grow hard, not wanting to, and fighting it, but there was nothing he could do.

I've wasted my time, Jack thought, as he tried to will his hard-on away. Made a long crawl and got eaten alive by mosquitoes and got nothing on him except that he likes poetry.

Jack thought the old man had nothing in his head except facts about fighting dogs and farming. What was he doing up there with that old woman when he was spending money to keep a young one in Memphis? Evelyn knew about the women. Everybody did. None of it made any sense.

Jack left them to their lovemaking and slipped back down the mound, crawling through cotton that in September would be harvested and the profits sent to the insurance company stockholders. Once a safe distance away he walked toward the lights of the house. When he glanced over his shoulder, he saw they had lit the lanterns again, two white spots in the thick darkness.

Probably up there talking about love, he thought. I'm smart enough to know love's not some goofy poem. It's getting a blowjob from a girl in a Memphis massage parlor.

They liked him there.

"You're young, you're clean, you come fast, and you leave a good tip," a girl had told him just last week.

Now he had no money for girls. No ribs at the Rendezvous. No more going to Ole Miss football games and spending the night with some planter's daughter at the Peabody Hotel.

He had almost reached the yard and saw Alligator sitting with his ears up, head held high as he sniffed the air.

Wonder if he smells that pussy out on the mound? Jack thought.

He unchained Alligator, who ran in a full circle around the house before he went inside. When Dexter kept other dogs, that would have meant a fight for sure. Later he lay in bed with Alligator asleep by the window, the dog's stink as much a part of the room as the smell of the peeling mahogany veneer on the furniture. The thought of the old man and Evelyn kept giving him a hard-on although he could not imagine why because it was not Evelyn he wanted. He guessed it was his wanting to be in Dexter's place, to put his hard cock where the old man thought none but his belonged.

Chapter Four

Dexter got up early and fixed a big breakfast: grits, a platter of scrambled eggs, biscuits with honey from their own hives, fig preserves on homemade bread, and bacon. Jack watched them eat as if they had been without food for a week.

"Have some of my bread," Dexter said, shoving the plate across the table to Evelyn.

She spooned preserves across a slice of bread.

"Dexter, you want to come over every morning and cook my breakfast?" she asked.

Dexter grinned and said, "Anytime."

Jack ate a biscuit with honey.

"Eat some grits before they get cold," Dexter said.

Jack put some on his plate but did not eat.

Dexter and Evelyn ate the rest of the bread and then went to work on the biscuits.

"It's smoking that stuff makes you feel bad in the morning," Dexter said.

"Take this last biscuit," Evelyn said.

Jack spread the biscuit with honey and ate part of it while Dexter and Evelyn cleared the table.

"Didn't you sleep good last night?" Dexter asked, sticking his head around the corner of the kitchen door.

"Slept fine," Jack said, wondering if Dexter knew he had spied on them.

30

Dexter's head disappeared. Then they were laughing in the kitchen.

Probably gonna screw her up against the refrigerator, Jack thought.

Jack sat on the steps, watching Alligator run the cable, the pulley singing on the wire. Alligator was methodical about it, always stopping just before the pulley ran out of free play. The screen door opened and closed.

"I want you to go up to Memphis for me," Dexter said.

He handed Jack a sealed manila envelope. It had "Sunset Apartments #24" written on it.

"What's this for?" Jack asked.

"Gambling debt," Dexter said. "Was poker last week. Money inside covers my losses. Take the dog with you. He's driving me crazy running the cable."

"I thought we were broke."

"I was planning on winning."

"I get it. One big pot. Say about a million. Then we buy the land back."

Instead of getting mad like Jack hoped, Dexter said, "There's a note in there to give you a fifty-dollar tip for bringing it. Not enough to buy any pussy with. But you can get drunk on it. Careful you don't let that dog chew somebody up."

Dexter went inside.

Out on Highway 61 with Alligator on the seat beside him, Jack drove north toward Memphis. He had thought about opening the envelope and seeing how much Dexter had lost, but written across the tape Dexter used to seal it was the word "DON'T."

Alligator stood on the seat and looked out the window. Jack too watched the fields pass, the land perfectly flat, with stands of cypress marking the creeks and swamps. The beans and cotton were up, the smell of pesticide in the air. He tried to calculate in his head how much a particular large field might bring its owner at the end of the summer when the crops were harvested.

He passed through Cleveland, looking at the new farm machinery for sale outside the dealers' showrooms: combines, pickers, tractors, irrigation systems. Occasionally he passed a crop-dusting service, the biplanes parked on the grass runway. He went up through Mound Bayou, Hushpuckena, and Clarksdale. The country was always the same: immense fields and patches of trees that marked the creeks.

In Memphis he followed Elvis Presley Boulevard and turned just before he reached Graceland. The Sunset Apartments were made of light brick built in the form of a square around a pool. There were the usual ornamental bushes planted in beds of pea gravel. The iron railing on the second story was painted white, but had been blackened in places by smoke from barbecue grills. The place smelled of chlorine and stale beer. When he knocked on number 24, no one answered.

"Hey," he heard someone yell from the pool.

She was lying on her stomach on a lounge chair.

"Is that for me?" she asked as she tied the straps to her top and ran up from the pool.

"I must have the wrong apartment building," he said as she stood before him, smelling of suntan oil.

She was a tall, blond-haired girl dressed in a string bikini and a pair of emerald earrings. He followed the curve of her inner thigh to where she had shaved herself so she would look good in the bottom. She knew he was looking. By her accent he guessed she came from some small town in Mississippi. But on a California beach she would be indistinguishable from the others until she opened her mouth.

He had spent three days with a girl who looked much like her when they had shipped him out at Oakland, her clipped western accent hard on his ears. She had tried to get him to desert, to go to Canada. But when he thought of the cold winters and the land waiting for him back in Mississippi, he had said no.

"Baby, that's my number on it," she said, snatching the envelope out of his hand. "Come on in," she continued as she opened the door. "You want a beer? There's plenty in the refrigerator." "I don't think that's for you," he said.

"What's your name?" she asked, tugging at the tape.

"Jack," he said.

"Why, I bet it is," she said with a smirk.

"I'm Amy. Some days I call myself Evonne or Angel when I'm in the mood."

There were piles of clothes thrown on the chairs and floor. New clothes, some with the price tags attached, were stacked on the kitchen table.

Jack wondered how he was going to get the envelope away from her. He hoped nobody was fooling with Alligator.

She got the envelope open and took out a roll of hundred-dollar bills. There was a note written in the old man's scrawl.

"Look, I made a mistake. My father owes somebody a gambling debt," he said.

"You're Dexter's son?" she said.

"Yeah."

"That son of a bitch. Says he won't pay my rent no more. Won't finish paying for my car." She crumpled up the letter and threw it across the room, her breasts bouncing against the top. "I gave up opportunities for him."

Jack started out of the apartment. This was Dexter's way of letting him know his crawl through the cotton the night before had not gone undetected.

"Wait a minute, baby," she said. "I'm not mad at you."

She closed the door.

"Let me go change," she went on. "Your daddy sent me a thousand dollars. We can have us a party." She went to the refrigerator and got him a beer and continued, "You sit down and wait while I get me a shower. You don't favor your daddy much, do you? Wouldn't have thought that old goat could have had such a good-looking son."

Jack wondered what this hooker was up to, tried to guess what she wanted. Some wanted you out the door after business was completed, but there were those who wanted to talk. They were trouble. This girl was one of those, but she had belonged to Dexter. Maybe she knew some things about the old man he could use?

He went and got Alligator because the dog could not stay out in the hot sun, chained in the bed of the truck to the ring he had welded to the bed. When he returned, she was sitting on the sofa reading a magazine, dressed in a pair of shorts and an Ole Miss T-shirt.

"I thought I'd scared you off," she said. Then she continued, "Honey, that's a big chain for a little dog."

"This is a fighting dog. Don't mess with him," Jack said.

He put Alligator in an empty bedroom.

She sat on the sofa beside him and told him she was from Olive Branch, Mississippi. Her father was an accountant. She had studied nursing.

"But I ended up giving massages and turning tricks instead," she said. "I was making more than the teachers. But some of those girls at school told on me. They kicked me out." She paused and played with her earrings. "You and your daddy don't get along."

"He tell you that?" Jack asked.

"Yes," she said.

"He makes it tough to like him," Jack said.

"Dexter treated me nice until today," she said. "But I was thinking of going back to nursing school. At Memphis State. Said he was going to help me."

Jack said, "You know what would really make him mad?"

"What's that?"

He put his beer can against the inside of her thigh. She squealed and jumped.

"Baby, you got a deal," she said. "But you be sure to tell him everything we did. You can make some of it up. I'll help. You won't be scared to tell?"

"I'm not scared of him," Jack said, wondering if this was what she had had in mind all along.

She shucked off her shorts and T-shirt, and regarded herself in a mirror on the opposite wall.

"I hate to be striped. I want an all-over tan," she said. "But I don't like tanning booths. It's like getting in a coffin. I need a private pool. Baby, you got one of those?"

"No," Jack said.

She kissed him, and he rolled her nipples between his fingers, thinking these were the same breasts that Dexter had fondled.

When he took off his shirt, she gasped at the sight of the shrapnel scars.

"A fight?" she asked.

"Vietnam," he said.

"I had a cousin killed over there," she said.

She traced the scars with her fingers.

"It's like there's something being spelled out on you," she said.

"Then it probably reads, 'Dumb.' I should have gone to Canada."

She reached for his cock and said, "I wish Dexter was here watching."

Jack laughed and said, "No, you don't."

For a moment he started to lose his hard-on at the thought of the old man but then she took him in her mouth.

"You're too big for this sofa," she said, taking his hand and leading him toward the bedroom.

He saw she had a king-size water bed. On one wall was a large framed photograph of Elvis and on the other a collection of ribbons.

"I was a swimmer in high school," she said. "I was good."

Jack looked at the water bed again.

"I don't like those things," he said.

"Baby, come on and try it," she said.

She put her hand on him and pulled him toward the bed.

"I'll get seasick," he said.

"You won't have time to be thinking about sea cruises," she said.

He lay down on the bed and instantly lost his hard-on.

"Baby, you won't drown," she said, and laughed.

She took him in her mouth again. Jack tried to lie perfectly still to keep the bed from moving. Nothing was happening. He did not feel sick at his stomach, just uncomfortable.

"Come on down on the floor," she said. "But it's me on top. You'll squash me."

She took him in her and made it last a long time. But he could not get the thought of Dexter out of his head and concentrate on her. She went first or pretended to. As she twisted on him, bringing him to the end, the figure of the old man kept appearing before him. And when he came, he had a clear picture in his head of Dexter peering at him as if through a window. He wondered if she was comparing his performance with Dexter's but knew better than to give her the edge by asking.

They went out to eat barbecue. Alligator sat between them as they rode in the truck.

Jack found a shady place to park the truck where they could watch it from the restaurant and chained Alligator in the bed. He was hungry and quickly ate three sandwiches, the meat firm and lean with little fat on it.

"I wish I could eat like that," she said. "I have to watch my weight." Then she continued, "I'll put this thousand dollars in the bank. Then enroll in the nursing school this summer. I had good grades. Could have my RN in a couple of years."

"No turning tricks on the side this time?"

"Not if you pick up my rent."

"Didn't the old man tell you? We're broke. Don't know where he got that thousand dollars."

"Then maybe just a little. Just to meet expenses. Last month I worked a bachelor party. Made three thousand in one night. That's how I got started not washing clothes. Easier and more fun to go out and buy new ones."

Jack decided not to ask her what the old man would think of her turning tricks while he was paying the bills. Maybe it was okay by him, part of the arrangement.

They went to Overton Park and walked Alligator, who wanted to run and kept tugging on the chain. Afterwards, Jack took his shirt off and lay in the shade of a big oak on the sweet-smelling new grass with Amy beside him. High in the top of the oak, the new leaves, outlined against the cloudless blue sky, quivered in the breeze. Lovers lay on blankets on the grass and from the road he heard the shouts of a busload of children.

Jack wished he could lie there the rest of the day. Once it grew dark he would talk Amy into making love on the grass.

But at Amy's insistence they went to a nightclub. They drank beer and watched people play shuffleboard as the place filled up for the night. A country-and-western band appeared. Amy hated country-and-western music.

"That ugly old thing Johnny Cash," she said. "Dresses in black all the time. Daddy plays his music till it makes me sick. Daddy don't even like Elvis."

Jack had never cared for music at all. He did not even have a radio in his truck. When he went on trips, he was content to sit and watch the countryside.

The band arrived and Amy tried to get them to play Elvis songs. But they refused and Amy sat at the bar and pouted. They danced when the band played something slow.

Jack had gone out to check on Alligator several times and found him asleep on a piece of old mattress in the back of the truck.

"Who owns that dog out in the green truck?" a man said to the bartender.

"Jack here does," Amy said.

"I got a dog that can whip that dog," the man said.

"There's not going to be any dogfights here, Lester," the bartender said.

Lester was a short little man, his thinning black hair slicked back. He was dressed in a pair of ostrich-skin boots and a cowboy shirt with pearl buttons. His chin came to a sharp point, and Jack guessed one punch on the chin would be lights-out for Lester.

"Well, then we can go someplace else," Lester said. "Fight 'em underneath the bridge."

"What kind of dog you got?" Jack asked.

"The meanest kind, a Doberman," Lester said. "He'll eat your little dog in two bites. Why, your dog can't weigh more than forty pounds."

Jack said, "There'll be no fight."

"Don't blame you for being scared," Lester said. "I've seen big fellers like you get sick at a fight." Lester looked Amy over good. "Little lady wouldn't like that."

Jack turned his back on Lester.

Lester pawed at his shoulder and whined, "You'd puke right on the floor."

"I got fifty dollars says my dog can pull that Volkswagen I saw parked out there," Jack said.

"I want to see a fight," Lester protested.

"Little dog can't pull my car," someone said.

"I got a hundred says he can," Amy said.

Then she whispered in Jack's ear, "Can he do it?"

"Easy," Jack whispered back.

Then Amy was covering everyone's bets.

They went out to the parking lot. Jack took Alligator out of the truck and connected his chain to the bumper of the car.

"Wait a minute," a woman said. "How far's he got to pull it?"

"Why, he'll pull it to Jackson if I ask him," Jack said.

"Twenty paces," Amy said.

Everyone agreed to this, and Amy paced them off.

Jack had seen Alligator pull loads in a cart Dexter kept at the house. But Dexter had never entered him in any weight pulls. As he stood outside the nightclub, smelling the trees and the river and the hot-tar scent of the asphalt, he wondered if Amy had made more bets than she would be able to cover.

Alligator did not look worried. He wagged his tail so hard it was a blur because he knew he was going to get to pull the car. He waited for Jack's command.

"Pull it, dog," Jack said, backing away from Alligator.

Alligator strained in the harness, the crowd silent. Amy crouched beside him, shouting encouragement. Alligator's claws scratched on the asphalt, the tendons in his legs swelling and making popping sounds. But the car did not move.

Amy ran over to Jack.

"You said he could pull it," she said. "Do something."

Jack knelt beside Alligator, who still strained to pull the car.

A trickle of foam came out of one side of Alligator's mouth, his yellow eyes stared straight ahead. The dog's stink filled the air, but Jack enjoyed filling his nostrils this time as if it were the scent of freshly turned earth.

"Pull it," Jack said, putting his hand on Alligator's back.

"No helping him," Lester said.

"He can't do it," someone said.

"Poor little thing," a woman said.

Jack felt Alligator's whole body drawn out taut. He could feel the dog's rage against the weight of the car. And he wanted to slip into the harness with Alligator.

"Pull it," he said, his face close to Alligator's ear.

Then he heard the car tires begin to turn, crunching against bits of broken glass and small pieces of gravel. The crowd started to scream.

"Take your hands off that dog!" Lester shouted.

Jack stood up and walked with Alligator as he steadily pulled the car across the line marked by beer bottles.

Amy threw her arms around Jack's neck. Alligator lay panting, belly to the asphalt. Jack was bending over to pick him up and Amy was collecting money from the losers, when he heard the sound of claws against the pavement.

"Get him!" Lester shouted.

Jack saw the Doberman coming and reached down to unsnap the swivel, but before he could touch it, Alligator was gone, the chain rattling on the asphalt. Alligator ran completely under the Doberman and went for a hold on a hind leg. The Doberman looked surprised that the smaller dog had not run from him. Jack heard the bones crunching as Alligator closed his jaws. The Doberman had now lost all interest in fighting and began to howl.

Lester began kicking Alligator, the dog ignoring him. The Doberman continued to howl, Alligator still working on his leg hold. Jack took a step toward them.

Pop, pop, pop, the sound went, as if somebody were shooting a cap gun. Jack saw the nickel-plated automatic in Lester's hand. He shot at Alligator but hit the Doberman twice in the neck. The dog growled and collapsed, the blood running out faster than Jack thought would have been possible. The crowd scattered, most of them lying flat on the asphalt. As Lester pointed the gun at Alligator, Jack caught him above the ear with his open hand. Lester toppled backwards. Alligator still had his leg hold on the dead Doberman.

Jack used the breaking stick to pry Alligator's jaws loose, and he and Amy left. His head felt clear now.

At her apartment Jack stood by the bed and watched her sleeping. She had promised to have the water bed replaced. He was pleased he had taken advantage of Dexter. And he tried to imagine what it was like for Dexter to lie in bed beside her, pressing his wrinkled old-man's body against her smooth young one. The scent of Alligator's semen drifted into his mind, and he decided Dexter would have to do it himself at the next collection. He wondered if Dexter had given her the picture of Elvis, an enlargement of his appearance at the Neshoba County Fair. A young singer then, his face contorted, hips grinding.

No, not that picture, he thought. No old man would give his mistress a picture of a young stud.

And he walked out of the bedroom thinking at last he had the edge on the old man. He felt like waking Amy up and making love to her again to celebrate. But then he paused, thinking that Lester could have easily shot him full of holes. Perhaps Dexter had known all along that this girl was going to be nothing but trouble, that he would be fool enough to get mixed up with her.

I don't care, he thought. Maybe it won't turn out the way he thinks.

Jack curled up on the couch with Alligator on the floor beside him on one of Amy's discarded sweaters. He had become excited at Alligator's victory over the Doberman, had felt Alligator's joy in battle as he bored under the Doberman and took the leg hold. Jack wondered what it would be like to handle Alligator in the pit against Blackmon's dog and if Dexter had somehow known all along that Alligator was going to fight when he sent them to Memphis.

He closed his eyes and tried to sleep, thinking this time not of night ambushes or booby traps but of the pit, of waiting for the referee's signal, his arms wrapped around Alligator.

Chapter Five

Jack helped them plant the marijuana between rows of corn in the rich dark soil that looked as if it would send the plants taller than a man in a few days. Norris turned out to drive a tractor and Blackmon directed the planting. Dexter refused to set foot on the island. Now the plants were up, and Norris was already counting his money.

Dexter never mentioned the gambling debt. Both pretended Jack had never taken the money to Memphis. At least once a week Jack went up to see Amy, who was now enrolled in school. She was still hooking on the side because as she said she had bills to pay and clothes to buy. She tried to dress like an Ole Miss sorority girl but gave herself away with the emerald earrings.

Jack once or twice almost asked her to stop turning tricks but caught himself just in time. He told himself he was visiting her just to get even with Dexter, that every time he slept with her he was getting closer to the time when the account between him and the old man would balance. But he found himself wanting to go to Memphis every day and when he got there he did not want to leave. He thought of love but told himself only a fool would fall for a hooker and decided it was just his eagerness to get even with Dexter.

And what made it so good was he was sure Dexter knew where he was going when he left for Memphis. One morning he found a shiny new padlock on the farm gas tank when he started to fill up his truck. He went to find Dexter.

"Why'd you put a new lock on the tank?" Jack asked.

"I thought somebody'd been stealing our gas," Dexter said. "You been using all that gas?"

"You know I have," Jack said.

"Memphis poontang," Dexter said. "Blackmon been giving you money?"

"I don't have to pay for it," Jack said, thinking about telling him right there about Amy.

"Boy, you be careful," Dexter said. "You may think it's free. There'll be the day you have to pay up."

Dexter handed him the key.

Jack wanted to scream at him that he was sleeping with Amy, the old man's former property. But he kept quiet. That would be just what Dexter wanted.

"I won't fall in love with some hooker," Jack said.

"Didn't say anything about love," Dexter said.

"You know all about love."

"No, never said that. How come you got love on your mind?"

Jack realized Dexter was playing with him.

"Love?" Jack said.

"It's not a dirty word," Dexter said.

Jack said, "What do you know about love? Wallowing in your dogs' blood. Humping every woman between here and Memphis."

Dexter smiled. "I'm trying. You're running from it. That's why some hooker's gonna skin you one of these days."

"No, I had you for a teacher. I know how to handle hookers."

Jack walked out of the room.

"Lock up the tank when you're through," Dexter called after him.

Jack wondered if he should stop seeing Amy as he drove north on 61, watching the rows of beans and cotton flash by, a pattern of black earth and green leaves. She hated and feared Alligator and asked Jack to leave him at home. They spent whole afternoons together in the park. He discovered she liked to make love outdoors.

Once in the darkness of early morning they made love on the diving board of the pool. Then she slipped into the pool.

"I want to do it in your daddy's bed," she said, treading water in front of him.

"Crazy," he said.

"Come on, baby," she said. "Think how mad he'd be."

"Mad enough to shoot both of us," he said.

She giggled and swam the length of the pool underwater, shooting up and onto the side in one smooth movement, like a seal at the Overton Park Zoo. She rested on the edge, dangling her legs in the pool while he sat on the diving board and put on his shorts.

"Put your clothes on," he said.

"You ol' sissy," she said.

She stood up and shook herself like a dog, pulling her wet hair back with both hands. He pulled his knees up to conceal his hard-on.

"Get dressed," he said.

"Right on ol' Dexter's bed," she said. "Then I'll be satisfied."

Blackmon called Jack on his CB radio from the island.

"Get out here quick," Blackmon said.

Jack crossed the lake in a johnboat and walked along the dirt track to the field. He liked walking into the trees where it was half-dark, the insects loud, shafts of sunlight streaming down. Birds called from the treetops. Grapevines hung from the trees and the rotting smell of wet vegetation made him think of the jungle. But the island was a good place, his mind filled with memories of listening to the dogs run on cold fall mornings.

He felt a farmer's pride in his crop when he walked out of the trees and saw the long rows of plants amid the taller corn. The field had not been worked billiard-table smooth as had those on the other side of the levee. It had a crest in the middle like the crown on a road and sloped away toward the southeast because that was where the water had drained back into the river during the last flood. But it was fertile, the high water leaving a layer of rich black topsoil. Crops needed much less fertilizer than those grown in fields protected from the fickleness of the river by the Corps of Engineers.

Blackmon, dressed in khaki work clothes, waited beneath the shade of a big cottonwood. Sweat bees hovered around his boots. The bearded catfisherman squatted with his back against the tree, cradling the same battered shotgun in his arms, the bluing worn off in places. His face was white instead of tan, the color of a fish belly. Jack imagined if he touched it, his fingers would push through the skin as if he had laid hands on a rotting corpse.

"Tudor here is making sure nobody snoops around this field," Blackmon said. "Deer been eating the crop."

Jack followed Blackmon and Tudor into the field. The plants were eight inches tall, but deer had eaten the tops off many of them, the soft dirt covered with deer tracks.

"Maybe if we planted enough to feed them too," Jack said.

"No, they'll get most of it if we don't do something," Blackmon said.

"Shoot 'em," Tudor said.

"Lots of folks won't like that," Jack said.

Blackmon said, "I don't care what they like. Too many deer anyhow. Breed like niggers."

"Some of those who hold small shares might pull out if we start shooting the deer," Jack said. "They kick up a big enough fuss over the antlerless season."

"Then what the hell are we going to do?" Blackmon asked.

"Fence 'em out."

"This is a big field."

"If the whole town turns out we can do it."

"Let me try a couple of things first."

Blackmon set guards in the field at night with lanterns to frighten away the deer. But they did not have enough manpower to cover the whole field, and deer continued to eat. They tried firing guns in the air, but the deer soon learned to ignore these and continued to browse on the tender plants.

They started on the fence, stringing it ten yards into the treeline so no one could see it from the air.

Bascomb Dodd came out to help for the first time. The preacher was a fat old man whose face was covered with red splotches that glowed even redder when he worked himself up during one of his sermons. Despite the heat he wore a dark polyester suit too tight across his chest.

Dodd took off his jacket and walked out into the field, bending over to look at one of the plants.

"No different from growing cotton," Blackmon said.

"I prayed for a new church," Bascomb said. "Is this his answer?"

"Don't know, Brother Bascomb," Blackmon said. "But it's mine."

The blacks from town arrived with a truckload of hog wire they were going to use for the fence. They had brought the truck across the lake on a barge.

"Earl, we got the wire. It's up to you to string it," Travis said.

"Travis, it's going to take all of us," Blackmon said.

Blackmon had given Travis a large share in exchange for keeping the blacks in line.

"I want to see everybody working," Travis said. "I want to see some of you white folks sweat." He looked up at the sky and said, "It's gonna be a hot one."

"I'm already sweating," Bascomb said. "Let's get to work. You people watch where you put your hands. They're crawling."

They started stringing, wrestling the wire through the mud and briars and nailing it with staples to the trees. Mosquitoes hummed in Jack's ears. Evelyn, dressed in work clothes, used a brush hook to cut the underbrush ahead of the stringers. She wore a .357 revolver in a holster on her belt. Dexter had taken the holster off a dead North Korean and the workmanship of the white leather was very fine. Jack had gotten sick of hearing the story about that ambush.

Evelyn's exploits with her pistol had become a local legend. She was a crack shot and loaded her own ammo. She carried it mostly on her fishing trips and used it to shoot snakes that sometimes became bold enough to try and steal the catch off her stringer. Once some of Tudor's kin had started easing their skiff into her favorite bream bed she had created by sinking Christmas trees in the lake. She pulled out the pistol and said, "You scull that boat one foot closer and I'll shoot your damn eyes out." Tudor's people understood threats like that and left her alone.

Jack was wrestling a piece of wire through a group of cypress knees when he saw it. It was too late to do anything but freeze. The cottonmouth, its body as thick as his forearm, had raised its head and now swayed back and forth between his legs like a snake charmer's cobra. It opened its mouth wide, displaying the glossy white lining. Jack had that same feeling he had always experienced at the start of a firefight, the instant when he felt unconnected to his body and seemed to be watching the rounds hit around him from some distant place and in slow motion. And then coming back to his body and falling to earth, hugging the contours. Now just as he struggled to move, his ears rang from the sound of the pistol. The snake's head disappeared.

Everybody laughed.

Jack sat down on a log and watched the headless snake twitch in the mud. The blood was red, but for such an animal he always thought it should be black or green.

"Got him with a one-fifty-grain Hydroshock," Evelyn said.

She was the perfect woman for Dexter, Jack thought. They could enjoy killing together.

But she did not like dogfighting. Dexter was going to have to work on that.

Jack worked with Travis, who talked about how they were going to use part of the profits for repairs on the school and books for the library. Jack was surprised how easily they had accepted the marijuana. Perhaps it was because their fathers and grandfathers had manufactured moonshine. But nobody did that anymore because of the high price of sugar.

When they broke for lunch, they had strung an eight-foot-high fence on one side of the field. Everyone was covered with mud from crossing a creek. Norris had hit himself on the hand with a hammer. The women came out with lunch, which they served on a cotton wagon.

Jack was starting to bite down on a piece of fried chicken when he noticed everyone was quiet. Bascomb was standing with his head bowed as he prepared to say the blessing.

Bascomb began, "Therefore God gave thee of the dew of heaven, and the fatness of the earth, and plenty of corn and wine."

He's going to preach a damn sermon, Jack thought.

Jack considered eating the drumstick anyway. Dexter would have already finished his chicken. Dexter and Bascomb had never got along.

"The Lord put those plants on the earth," Bascomb said. "And he put the deer on this earth to eat them. And he put man on this earth to fence out the deer."

The patches on Bascomb's face glowed red.

"Lord bless this field, these good people, and bless their axes, staples, wire, brush hooks, wagons, trucks, and boats." He paused and wiped his face against his shirtsleeve before he continued, "And bless these plants which you have given to us."

"Amen, Brother," a black man said.

"The food, Brother Bascomb," Evelyn said. "The food."

Bascomb looked confused for a moment before he said, "Yes, Lord, bless this food."

He sat down and one of the women started to pour him a cup of ice tea. Instead Bascomb took the pitcher from her and drained half of it in a series of big gulps.

Evelyn sat down beside Jack. She used a whetstone to sharpen her brush hook.

"Dexter wouldn't come," she said, the stone singing against the blade.

"He thinks we're all fools," Jack said. "Thinks you're a fool too."

"He plans on making money off Alligator," she said. "I wish he would get rid of that dog."

"That's what Mother used to say," Jack said. "Didn't listen to her either."

"Don't be so hard on your father," she said, testing the edge with her finger.

Jack said, "Just wait. You'll find out what he's like."

"I know what Dexter's like. He has my heart."

Jack brushed a mosquito away from his ear and said, "Then marry him. I don't care. Invite his whores to the wedding."

Evelyn said, "Dexter's right. There's no use talking to you."

She got up and walked off, carrying the brush hook over her shoulder.

"You'll see," Jack called after her. "He doesn't care about anybody. No different from Alligator."

She kept walking, and Jack lay back on the ground. From the river, only a quarter of a mile away, came the whistle of a towboat. He noticed trash caught up in a tree ten feet above his head from the high water five years before. Dexter might have been right about that.

How could any woman fall in love with Dexter? he thought.

He thought of Amy. At least he had gotten the better of the old man there.

"Back to work," Blackmon said.

Evelyn was already chopping brush. He heard the steady chink of the brush hook as it cut through cane, briars, and saplings.

After three days they had eight feet of wire around the field. They barbecued a pig in celebration at the riverboat. Travis and his people held their own celebration at the county school, where he was principal. Only the blacks and the children of the catfishermen went there now, the children of the white farmers in private schools. After it grew dark and Bascomb left, they broke out a keg of beer.

The people Jack's age began to play Rolling Stones, Beach Boys, Beatles, and Smokey Robinson records. Blackmon and his friends went up to the pilothouse to drink while the young people danced. Norris was very drunk, reliving with Sally Ann fraternity parties at Ole Miss.

Jack had spent a year at Mississippi State studying agriculture. After his mother left, he quit and came home to farm.

"I want to farm," he had told Dexter.

"Fine," Dexter said. "You got any land?"

"Our land."

"Mine, go back to school."

But he refused and was drafted.

He watched Norris and Sally Ann and thought of Amy. Fooling with her was just as stupid as quitting school and getting drafted.

Jack left the party and went out on the deck, walking to the bow. He heard Blackmon laughing from the pilothouse. He sat down on one of the twin ladders that led to the hurricane deck and wished they were out on the big river. The *Nathan B.* was still seaworthy. She had been built in Cincinnati for the Ohio and upper Mississippi trade with a steel hull and coal-fired boilers. Now the boilers were gone, replaced by diesel engines. Then her name had been the *Roscoe Smith,* but after the trade collapsed she was sold to the Corps of Engineers, who used her as a supply boat. They were going to cut her up for scrap in New Orleans when Dexter and his friends saved her.

He thought how peaceful it would be out on the big river, watching the sun come up over a different shoreline every morning, everything clean and shot through with the morning light. And at night he could count the lights on the shore, Vicksburg and Natchez hills of lights, and then down to New Orleans. He could get a job on an offshore oil rig and forget about Amy and the land that was no longer his.

After the party broke up, Blackmon wanted to go check on the fence. He could not reach Tudor on the radio.

They all climbed into a big johnboat. Evelyn ran the motor and Norris and Sally Ann sat in the middle. Blackmon sat in the bow next to Jack. Norris was very drunk, and Sally Ann kept trying to make him put on a life jacket, but he refused.

There was no moon, and timber on the island rose before them as a dark line against the sky. No one spoke. Even Norris had shut up. The motor droned, and Jack smelled gas mixed with the scent of oil. Water sloshed about at his feet from a small leak. Blackmon turned on his eight-cell flashlight to locate the landing, and the instant the light came on they all began to talk at once. Norris wanted a kiss from Sally Ann.

"Not here," she kept saying.

Norris lost his balance and fell into the bottom of the boat. Sally Ann tried to get him back on the seat.

"Let him lay there and sleep it off," Blackmon said.

At the landing they got Norris out of the boat, but he was too drunk to walk. Sally Ann and Evelyn stayed with him while Jack and Blackmon went to check on the fence. Blackmon played the light at their feet, on the lookout for snakes. Insects buzzed and clicked from the trees.

They reached the field, and Blackmon turned the flashlight on the plants. Eyes glowed red in the light and then the deer ran, white tails flashing, taking the fence in graceful bounds and disappearing into the dark trees.

"Shit," Blackmon said. "I knew we should've built it higher."

They organized another building party and added four feet to the fence, topping it with three strands of barbed wire. The undamaged plants were doing well, some growing as much as an inch a day. But Blackmon guessed the deer had already ruined almost twenty percent of the crop.

Jack and Blackmon went out to check on the field. When Blackmon turned on the light, nothing moved, the plants motionless under the star-filled sky, waiting for the sun to come up so they could tap the light and grow. Later in the summer they would produce the resin that was going to buy back their land. Jack longed to see the heavy top colas form, covered with resin glands.

The plants had a ranker smell than the corn. Blackmon noticed Jack sniffing the air.

"That's the smell of money," Blackmon said. "Won't be like cotton or beans that cost more to grow than sell." Blackmon went on, "Your daddy's been talking about a fight this fall. You gonna handle Alligator?"

"No," Jack said.

"Your daddy says Alligator's dead game. You believe that?"

"Yes."

"He might be dead game for you but not for Dexter."

Jack did not reply. Blackmon was a dark shape beside him. He could smell the sweat on the man and the scent of his tobacco.

Blackmon said, "Your daddy's talking about Alligator fighting my Firecracker. Sounds like he wants Alligator dead. Can he whip a dog outweighs him twenty pounds?"

Jack now wished he had told Blackmon nothing.

"Put your money up," Jack said.

Blackmon laughed. "Why, you're Dexter's son after all. Wouldn't surprise me to see you in the pit."

Jack wished Amy were with him. Did she have his heart? Amy would like the idea of making love among the plants or better yet on a river sandbar, the sand squeaking beneath their bodies, the river sliding by deep and powerful in the dark.

He followed Blackmon into the trees.

Chapter Six

A mockingbird singing in the big sycamore that shaded the house woke Jack in the morning. The bird sang as if its heart were about to burst, but instead of the song building to some climax it went on and on, the bird repeating the same notes.

The fields were covered with a morning fog, so he could not see the levee or even the Indian mound. All about the yard spiderwebs were beaded with a heavy dew. He got up and put Alligator on the cable. Immediately Alligator began running back and forth, pausing and panting for a few seconds between laps like an athlete running wind sprints. Dexter's truck was gone, so Jack went to the kitchen to fix his own breakfast.

He heard tires on the gravel, which he guessed was Dexter returning. Then Alligator stopped running the wire. He looked out the kitchen window and saw Amy standing on the grass. Alligator lay with his belly to the grass, hind legs stretched out behind him. She took several steps and stopped, looking small and fragile in a sundress and a pair of white sandals. Another step would bring her within Alligator's reach.

Jack started for the door.

"Stop!" he yelled.

He ran, the grass cold and wet against his bare feet, listening to the mockingbird singing of love, of new life, as if they were in a world in which fighting dogs were not permitted. She took a step backward and Alligator made his move, the pulley singing on the cable. Jack felt as if he were running in sand, his feet mired in the

53

grass, feeling the blades between his toes and pieces of spiderweb. He watched Alligator move toward her, girl and dog frozen before his eyes with wisps of fog drifting about them, and he knew he was not going to be able to reach her. But Alligator came up short, his jaws snapping at the edge of her sundress.

She did not scream, but her face went white.

"Are you crazy? Dexter could be back here any minute," he said.

"No, he's headed for Greenville. I followed him for a couple of miles," she said.

"That dog could have killed you," he said. "You remember that. Stay away from him. I thought you didn't like him."

"I don't. He stinks. I just wanted to look at him."

She started to cry. He put his arm around her, but she pushed him away.

"Don't touch me," she said.

"Come on in the house," he said.

"No, I'm going home."

"You drove all the way from Memphis. Can't leave now."

"You got that dog. You don't need me."

"Come on inside."

"You want me to stay?"

"Sure."

One of the straps had slipped off her shoulder, and her eyes were red from crying. The mockingbird had stopped singing, and the fog was beginning to break up, patches of blue appearing overhead.

He took a deep breath and said, "You have my heart."

"That's the sweetest thing," she said.

She threw her arms around his neck and kissed him.

And you're a fool for saying it, Jack thought to himself.

She came into the kitchen and drank coffee while he fixed them scrambled eggs, sausage, and biscuits. She ate twice as much as he did.

"What about your diet?"

"I'm running every day now and swimming laps. I'm taking a fitness class at school."

She walked all over the house, asking him questions about various rooms. She was especially interested in the liquid-nitrogen refrigerator.

Finally she looked at Dexter's room. His mother's dressing table with its thin legs and the ivory inlaid top was gone. In its place was a gun safe for Dexter's fine shotguns and rifles. The room smelled of gun oil and tobacco. On the walls were pictures of Dexter's best dogs. She sat down on the bed.

"Right now," she said. "He'd drive off the road if he knew."

"No, not here," Jack said.

He thought of his mother sleeping by Dexter's side for twenty years.

"Come on, baby," she said.

"Don't call me that," he said.

She giggled and slipped out of her sundress. He walked out of the room, going to the kitchen, where he started to clean up the breakfast dishes. She came into the kitchen wearing Evelyn's silk kimono.

"I'm sorry," she said.

She took his hands and put them inside the kimono. Jack smelled Evelyn's perfume on the silk.

"Did you come down here to see me or to get even with my daddy?" Jack asked.

"For you," she said.

"I want you to stop working."

"Don't ask me to do that."

"Why?"

"I'm no hooker. I'm going to be a nurse. I can quit anytime I want. Besides, it keeps me free."

"You sound like my daddy. He talks about being a free man all the time. You learn that from him?"

"Why do you keep bringing up your daddy? I thought you hated him."

"I want you to quit."

She shook her head, the emerald earrings swaying.

Jack thought that this was his chance to shut up, to stop before he got in any deeper. But as he held her breasts, he felt tied to her by something stronger than Alligator's chain.

"I'll take care of you," he said.

"With what?" she asked. "You're broke."

So he told her about the marijuana.

"By the time Ole Miss plays LSU, we'll have plenty of money," he said.

She said, "I won't become the property of any man. I can quit hooking anytime I want. In two years I'll be a nurse. I can make good money."

"I won't stop loving you."

"I can't love anyone."

"You can love me."

"No, it's too late."

He placed two fingers against her lips.

"Hush," he said. "I'll take care of you."

"I'm crazy, Jack. Sometimes, I wish Memphis would slide off into the river and me with it."

"I won't let anything happen to you."

"You won't. Will you stay with me when I feel bad? I'll say mean things to you."

"I won't pay any attention to them."

"You won't be able to trust me."

"I don't care."

She kissed him, and as she pressed up against him, twisting her pelvis against his hard-on, he did not think of Dexter or revenge but only that he wanted to hold on to her and not let go.

"I'll be bad for you," she continued.

"No, good," he said.

"Let's get away from here. We could go to New Orleans or California."

"This is my home. I'll buy back Daddy's land."

"You'll get caught."

"No, it's all fixed."

"Tell me nothing's going to happen."

"It'll be fine."

"My daddy's not an accountant. He drives a garbage truck in Memphis."

"My old man fights dogs."

"I could be lying to you. Sometimes I don't even know if I'm telling the truth."

"Once I get our land back everything'll be fine. We'll have a house of our own. We'll have children."

"I don't know if I would be a good mother."

"You'll be a good mother."

"Say that again."

"You'll be a good mother."

They went to his bed.

"I can smell that dog," she said.

He took a fan and set it in the window.

"Why don't you have air-conditioning?" she asked. "Your daddy's rich."

"He says air-conditioning is going to cause the destruction of civilization," Jack said.

She laughed. "You can't have much civilization if it's too hot to wear clothes."

Then she lay back on the bed.

"You do me, baby," she said.

"I thought you weren't going to call me that," he said.

She laughed.

"I have to think up some name," she said.

"What about Jack?" he asked.

"Jack, do me first," she said. "I've done you enough."

He hesitated, and she laughed.

"It's all right. And from now on it'll be nobody but you."

He kissed her thigh, her hands stroking his back and head. Her hair tickled his nose.

The pistol went off, six shots in quick succession. She screamed and sat up, causing him to bump his nose against her pelvis. He heard the cans falling. It was Evelyn, shooting cans off a board she had set up on the top of two fence posts. She had probably come looking for Dexter and, seeing his truck was gone, decided to wait for him. They both liked to target-shoot. She could hit clay pigeons thrown with a hand trap, but Dexter could not.

"She won't come in the house," Jack said.

But Amy was already putting on her clothes.

"Put that robe back where you found it," Jack said. "That's hers."

They went out on the porch. Evelyn saw them and walked up from the yard. She wore her ear protectors around her neck. Jack told her that Dexter had gone to Greenville.

Jack went to get them all a beer. Evelyn was already inquiring into Amy's family and Amy was lying, telling Evelyn her father was a lawyer in Memphis. Jack drank his beer fast, listening to Amy tell Evelyn about her house on Peabody and how much she had enjoyed last season's Cotton Carnival.

"Dexter never told me you were seeing somebody regular," Evelyn said.

"Maybe he forgot," Jack said.

Jack could tell that Amy and Evelyn liked each other. But he wondered how Evelyn was going to like Amy when she found out who she was, and sooner or later Evelyn was going to find out.

Evelyn left and they went back inside. This time they were not interrupted although Jack expected that any minute Dexter was going to drive up.

He had a hard time persuading Amy to leave. She walked over the house again, asking him questions about what it was like growing up there. She had him take one of the straws out of the liquid-nitrogen refrigerator.

"Looks like a frozen milkshake," she said.

"Daddy's going to be getting back," he said, taking her out onto the front porch.

The fog was gone, the sky without a cloud. It was already hot.

"What would he do?" she asked.

"Don't know," he said.

"He was nice to me."

Jack wished he had never seen her.

"Don't talk about him," he said.

She said, "It was just business."

He hated her and Dexter, wished Alligator had gotten her. But then the thought of Alligator's jaws closing around any part of that brown body caused him to tremble.

"You all right?" she asked, putting her hand on his arm.

"Fine," he said.

"You've been sweet to me."

"You've got to leave."

"Say it again."

"What?"

"About me having your heart."

Amy looked good in the sundress, those long brown legs, her earrings catching the light and turning it green. She pressed up against him, her hands around his neck.

"You have my heart," he said.

"That's so sweet," she said. "That's the sweetest thing anybody's ever said to me. Usually they want me to talk dirty or listen to them talk dirty. You make me feel clean."

"I'm just one of them?"

"No, you know you're not," she said. "Don't you ever say that."

"Go on now."

She kissed him and walked out to her car while he remained on the porch. The light was caught up in her hair as she walked through the heat, which now lay heavy on the land, and the bird began to sing again, pouring out the liquid notes that hung frozen in the humid air.

He wished her gone before Dexter returned, but at the same time wanted her to stay so the old man would know he was beaten.

Chapter Seven

J ack watched Dexter and the old black man stand before
Alligator, who lay panting from the heat under the shade of
his shelter, the piece of unpainted plywood split and warped
from the rain and sun. The men were like worshipers struck
dumb by the sight of their god, while around them the sweat bees
whined. Alligator snapped at one that flew too close to his head.
The black man spat on the grass and studied the patterns. Dexter
did the same.

"He's some dog, ain't he?" Dexter said.

"He's a good one," Dumas said.

Dumas was Dexter's trainer. He had not worked Dexter's corner
for a long time. But in the old days he was always there during a
tough fight.

"Don't like to do much with 'em in this heat," Dumas said.

"We're fighting before Halloween," Dexter said.

"Be better to wait until winter," Dumas said. Then he turned to
Jack. "Are you gonna be in the corner?"

"No," Jack said.

"He don't care much about his family's land," Dexter said.

"I'll have the money to buy it back before you will," Jack said.

"You can speak to that dog," Dumas said to Jack.

"You're too smart to believe that," Jack said.

They had moved out of the sun under the shade of a pecan as if
they did not want to risk being overheard by Alligator.

"Dog'll fight for you till his heart swells up and busts," Dumas
said.

"You talk to him," Jack said. "That dog don't have a heart. Devil left it out when he made him."

"Jack'll help in the training," Dexter said.

"I'll do that," Jack said. "Just don't expect to see me in the corner."

Dexter and Dumas smiled at each other.

"You think I'm going to be there, but I'm not," Jack said.

They kept grinning.

"Bring him out to me in the morning," Dumas said to Jack. "We need to get started."

Dumas lived with his wife, Carrie, on a barge he had converted into a houseboat, anchored in an old creek channel that cut through one end of the island. He had built the big two-story cabin after the style of a riverboat, and trimmed with gingerbread woodwork the cabin looked like the hurricane and texas decks of an old side-wheeler. Dumas still worked for Dexter, watching out for poachers on the island. They liked to come down the river from Memphis during deer season. He took the points and plugs out of their motors, leaving them stranded. Then they had to appear before Dexter, who was justice of the peace.

Jack woke early and put Alligator in the truck. The sun was just rising when he crossed the levee, and the crop dusters were begin-ning to work the field as they always did in the early morning before there was any wind. A red biplane made a slow turn just above the treetops as he crossed the cattle guard made of steel pipe set in the road at the foot of the levee. He wished he were up there in the clean air, fields and lake and river and Alligator far below. At the riverboat he transferred Alligator to a johnboat and started up the lake.

The surface, covered with patches of mist, was like a piece of polished black metal. Alligator stood motionless in the bow, as if he too were made of iron, and looked up the lake, occasionally turning his head to follow the flight of birds flushed out of the shoreline trees.

"What you thinking, dog?" Jack said.

Alligator raised his ears but did not turn his head to look at him.

Jack wondered if what Dumas said was true about his being able to talk to Alligator. He still believed having the dog around him all the time gave him an advantage over Dexter, but he was worried that he had grown used to the dog's stink, no longer smelled it in the bedroom. He sensed Alligator knew he was about to begin training for battle. Maybe knowing things like that about the dog was what Dumas had meant?

He reached the mouth of the slough and turned the boat into it, steering among the snags and cypresses. Dumas was standing on deck waiting. Jack lifted Alligator up to him and then climbed aboard. The barge was covered with flowering plants. Roses grew in boxes. Jessamine and trumpet creeper covered the rail. Carrie had trained honeysuckle up the posts that supported the texas deck. A muscadine vine hung over one side, almost touching the water, the vine already covered with green grapes. The sweet smell of flowers filled the air. She also raised greens and tomatoes in dirt-filled boxes.

"Carrie is frying a mess of crappie for breakfast," Dumas said. "Come and eat."

Jack ate the sweet crappie, the tender meat flaking off the bones. They drank black coffee thick with cream.

Carrie always kept an eye on Alligator.

"How come you bringing that dog around here?" she asked Dumas.

"Training," Dumas said.

"Fighting," Carrie said. "I don't mind them serpents." She pointed to a heap of canvas sacks next to the railing. "And I don't mind them other dogs. But that dog has got the curse on him."

"She likes the buzzing snakes better than dogs," Dumas said.

"Snakes are just being snakes," she said. "But that dog's being what he ain't supposed to be."

Dumas made part of his living by catching rattlesnakes and selling their venom to pharmaceutical companies. At the other end of the barge was a row of cages where he kept snakes he was milking. Usually he milked the snakes and returned them to the woods. He claimed he could find a particular snake anytime he wanted. He also ran trotlines and hoop nets. He guided hunters who came for deer and razorbacks. Dumas had raised three sons on the barge. All of them had graduated from high school. Two were in the Marines. The only one Jack knew well was Luther, who was playing football for Ole Miss.

Alligator trotted over and sniffed at the sacks. Then he backed off.

"They won't stick their tusks in you," Carrie said. "Afraid they might get poisoned." Then she said to Dumas, "What you gonna do with all them snakes? You know they're not buying poison right now." And turning to Jack she continued, "He's been milking snakes all morning. One of these days he's gonna get hisself bit."

Dumas laughed.

"I been taking poison for thirty years now. Old woman puts it in my coffee," Dumas said.

Jack glanced at his half-empty cup.

Dumas continued, "Why, a snake would go belly-up in five minutes if he bit me."

"And I been living out here with a crazy man all those years," she said. "Tell Dexter's boy about the time a sack of serpents got loose in the bedroom. We were sitting on the bed in the dark, listening to 'em shaking their bells and crawling."

"I finally got the lantern lit," Dumas said. "It was easy after that." He smiled at Carrie and said, "We didn't go back to sleep."

"Hush, now," she said, and laughed.

Dumas said, "Won't happen like that again. Now we got a generator. Have electric lights just like in town."

They finished eating and put Alligator into Dumas's wooden skiff, which he had built himself out of cypress boards. Dumas took the oars and Jack sat with Alligator next to him.

"Get in there with the snakes and turtles," Jack said to Alligator.

The dog went over the side without hesitation and swam in circles around the boat.

Dumas rowed up the lake at a steady pace. Alligator followed.

"We'll work him about a quarter of a mile today," Dumas said. "Won't overheat in the water."

Jack turned his back to Dumas and watched Alligator swim. He believed Alligator would continue to swim until he wanted him to stop. Swim all the way to China. It was not something he would have to say to the dog. Alligator knew, and he knew. That was why Dexter wanted him in the pit.

Alligator was the most dangerous thing in the lake, worse than some hundred-pound snapping turtle lying in the mud on the bottom. More deadly than the biggest moccasin. And it was all because Alligator had hot blood running in his veins, not some thin, cold watery stuff. Alligator could love and hate.

But what was his connection with the dog? Why did Alligator want to please him?

Was it love, the stuff of dog stories he had read when he was a boy? That was not it. The dog wanted something from him. He shuddered at the thought of looking at the world through the dog's eyes, ignoring pain or maybe not even acknowledging that it existed. Living to fight.

"Let's get him in the boat," Dumas said.

Jack pulled him over the side and Alligator shook, spraying water on them. He sat in the bow and began to lick himself dry.

"That dog smells like a skunk," Dumas said.

"You could swim him all day long and he'd still smell," Jack said.

"He worked good for you," Dumas said.

"Why?"

"Don't know. Did you raise him?"

"No."

"Some dogs just latch on to a person."

"I don't even like him."

Alligator shook himself again and stood up, his head toward the trees, his ears raised.

"Sure you do. He knows it," Dumas said. "See how good he worked."

"I'm not going in the pit," Jack said.

"I know. But he works good in training. Fights are won in training."

"Then we'll train him good."

"How come your daddy wants to match him against that Firecracker dog?"

"Breeding rights."

And Jack told Dumas about the liquid-nitrogen refrigerator and the semen collections.

"Alligator's good but not that good. Twenty pounds is too much to give up. Won't be able to snatch up that dog and bite clean through his backbone."

"Then he'll lose. Dexter'll have shot his wad."

"Maybe so."

Dumas paused, pulling on the oars, which creaked in the oarlocks.

"That Firecracker dog'll go for the leg. The stifle," Dumas said, pointing at the joint in Alligator's hind leg. "He gets a good hold there, it'll be over. Dog like Alligator depends on being quick to win. The fight'll be just starting, but it'll be over. Three hours is what I guess. Alligator won't give up."

Jack wondered why he should care if Alligator got killed. Just as long as he did not have to take part in it.

"What that dog needs is an edge," Dumas said.

"How?" Jack asked. "Daddy'll be mad if you do anything."

Some handlers tried to cheat by putting poison or some badtasting substance on their dogs.

"I've been hired to train and handle a dog," Dumas said. "I don't plan on losing."

"Blackmon's too smart for any cheating," Jack said.

"Well, we'll train him good. That's the best way."

Back at the barge Dumas threw a rope with a piece of truck inner tube tied to it over the limb of a big oak. Jack had Alligator take the inner tube in his mouth. They pulled him up and let him hang suspended for a count of ten. Then they lowered him and let him pull on the inner tube before hoisting him again, the muscles in his neck bulging. Jack wondered if Alligator would land on his feet like a cat if he fell.

Then they fed him. It was commercial dog food out of a sack. Carrie poured broth over it, and Dumas added a liquid out of a small blue bottle.

"What's that?" Jack asked.

"Vitamins," Dumas said. "We used to think red meat was what to get them ready with. Learned we was wrong about that."

Alligator sniffed at the food and walked away.

Dumas said, "Tell him to eat."

"Go on, dog," Jack said.

Alligator returned to the bowl and ate in his usual, unhurried manner.

"We'll swim him once a day for a while," Dumas said. "I want you to talk to him. Make a fuss over him. Pretend he's a girl you're sweet on."

"How come you never made a fuss over me?" Carrie asked.

"Honey, I made the biggest fuss you ever saw," Dumas said. "You getting too old to remember?"

"I remember," she said, and they both laughed.

"Let that dog sleep some and you can take him back late this evening when it gets cool," Dumas said.

Jack sat in an arbor where Carrie had trained morning glories and roses to climb over a wood frame. The sweet smell covered the stink of Alligator, who slept at his feet. At the other end of the barge Dumas was milking snakes. Every now and then he heard a rattler shake his bell. Bees worked the flowers, and a hummingbird, the sunlight playing off different shades of its glossy green head feathers, darted about.

He felt good and wished Amy were with him. But just as he was settling into a dream of her, Alligator got up and shook himself, a fine spray of water falling on Jack and the flowers, the stink rising from the dog's damp coat.

Chapter Eight

Jack walked out of Mr. Francis's store eating a piece of beef jerky, when he saw Evelyn waving at him from the courthouse lawn. He strolled across the deserted street. They met next to the statue of the Confederate soldier who gazed unblinking into the afternoon sun, rifle in hand, bedroll slung across his back, while sparrows perched on the brim of his hat. The courthouse was in bad shape. They had had it half finished when the war started, and although it had not been burned, times were never good enough to finish the job. A set of double doors on the second floor led to a balcony that had never been built.

They went inside to her office, the marble-floored foyer smelling of cigar smoke and chewing tobacco. Twenty years before Uncle Charles Musson, his mother's brother, had begun painting murals of the journey of Hernando de Soto through the county. But Dexter had introduced Uncle Charles to dogfighting, and the artist had become fascinated with the sport. He had gotten drunk and on the wall painted a pit bull fight scene: two giant dogs locked in combat. He was fired and now lived in New Orleans.

"Good artist but crazy like all the Mussons," Dexter liked to say.

A housepainter was hired to paint over the dogfight pictures, leaving blank gaps between the half-completed figures of the mural. A robed, legless priest gestured with his cross toward a white space. De Soto, dressed in shining cuirass and plumed helmet, lifted his sword against an unseen enemy.

"Blackmon wants us out at the field," she said.

Evelyn was dressed in her mayor's outfit. She looked good, and he did not blame Dexter for liking her. But then he thought of his mother and felt disgust with both her and Dexter.

"What's it this time?" he asked.

"The plants are dying," Evelyn said. "Blackmon called me."

"Well, we can't have the county agent or somebody from Mississippi State come up to look at them," Jack said.

Evelyn laughed.

"Not unless we all want to go to jail," she said as she gathered up a bundle of clothes.

He waited in the office while she changed. From the window he could see Alligator chained in the truck with two small boys watching him and the dog ignoring them. The boys knew better than to get too close.

They drove out of town now and headed for the levee. Alligator was curled up asleep, tired from a long swim in the lake. Jack wondered if Dexter had told her he had spied on them that night at the Indian mound. But he was not sure Dexter knew he was there. No, he would not have told Evelyn.

"Dexter says you should bring that nice girl home to dinner," Evelyn said. "I'll come over and cook."

Jack wondered if Dexter knew it was Amy. But there was no way for him to know and Jack felt safe. Amy had told Evelyn her name was Mary Ann.

"I've got to be careful about the girls I bring around him," Jack said.

Evelyn looked at a field of cotton.

"Nice crop," she said.

They went past the catfishermen's shacks. Jack tried to think of something else to say to make her mad.

"I think a lot of Dexter," Evelyn said. "I liked your mother."

Jack hit the brakes hard, the truck sliding to a stop at the foot of

the levee in a cloud of brown dust. Alligator woke up and stuck his
head through the window. A herd of cows grazing on the side of
the levee raised their heads.

"Probably appreciates what you're doing with him," Jack said.

"Dexter and I were thinking about getting married once,"
Evelyn said. "He went to Korea. When he came home, things
weren't the same."

"He never told me," Jack said.

"There's lots of things you don't know," Evelyn said.

"Like what?"

"About why your mother left."

"That's easy. He was humping everything in a skirt between
here and Memphis."

"It's not that simple."

They had crossed the levee and were in the woods.

She continued, "Listen to me. Margaret was always flighty.
Even when we were children. She made things hard on a man like
Dexter. Talk to him about her."

Jack had heard the stories about his mother, about how she had
her lovers too. The first time a drunken crop duster repeated them
in his hearing he gave the man a beating that kept anyone from ever
mentioning to him again the lies spread by Dexter.

"You and him are the perfect pair," Jack said. "He can fight the
dogs, and you can shoot them if they lose."

"Talk to him," she said.

"We're through talking," Jack said. "You remember that girl
you met? She was his whore and him old enough to be her father.
Would still be seeing her but he ran out of money to pay for it.
That's how I met her. Sent me up to pay her off."

Jack wished he had kept his mouth shut. Now she would tell
Dexter. But that was all right because it would make Dexter mad.
Maybe Evelyn would not have anything further to do with the old
man.

Evelyn looked straight ahead as if she were trying to pretend she
was the only one in the truck.

She turned back to him and said, "I love Dexter. I'd be careful with that girl. Does she know about the marijuana?"

"She knows," Jack said. "But she'll keep her mouth shut."

"I hope so," Evelyn said. "Be careful with her. She doesn't like other women. Knows they're on to her tricks. Those kind are dangerous."

"You're the one that needs to watch out. The old man hasn't exactly got a history of being faithful."

"I know him better than you."

"Good luck," Jack said, thankful she was taking it so well and had not started crying.

Evelyn ran the boat while Jack sat with Alligator. The sun hung low over the trees, but it was still very hot, the lake shining under the light as if it were molten metal poured out on the flat land to puddle and cool. Nothing was moving, no birds in the sky, no fish rising to take insects. Not even the splash of a gar gulping air broke the stillness. Alligator panted and Jack splashed handfuls of warm lake water on him, the stink rising from his coat.

Blackmon met them when they reached the island. They walked along the dirt track to the field. Jack was thankful for the coolness of the trees, the powder-fine dust rising in spurts under his boots. Insects whined from the trees.

"The plants are dying," Blackmon said.

"From what?" Evelyn asked.

"Don't know," Blackmon said.

They came out of the trees into the field. Not all the waist-high plants had been affected, but Jack could see whole sections of the field, some as large as an acre, where the lower leaves were beginning to curl up and turn brown.

Inside the fence, Evelyn examined the plants. Then she shook a plant, and what looked like a miniature snowstorm fell from its leaves.

"Whiteflies," Evelyn said. "They get in my garden this time of year. Suck the juice out of the leaves."

She pulled a leaf off and showed them the white speckling on the underside.

"We'll have to spray with malathion," she said.

"Didn't give Robert a share," Blackmon said. "We'll have to do it now."

Robert Red was a crop duster who flew off a small grass airstrip halfway between Stringtown and Greenville. He had flown choppers in Vietnam. Robert drank too much. When stationed as an instructor at Fort Rucker, he landed a chopper at the fifty-yard line just before the Auburn-Alabama game. That finished his army career.

"He'll get drunk and tell everybody in Memphis," Evelyn said.

"We won't tell him what he's dusting," Blackmon said.

"No, he smokes the stuff," Evelyn said. "He'll know."

"We've got to do something quick," Blackmon said. "Some of those plants won't recover."

"Get somebody else," Jack said.

Evelyn said, "No, we need to keep this close to home. We let somebody we don't know in, and they'll want more than we can afford to give."

"When I grow beans and cotton, I know what to spray for," Blackmon said, kicking at a dead plant. "Pests'll get the whole crop."

Blackmon's hat had fallen off as whiteflies swarmed around him from the plants he had kicked. He pulled up a plant by the roots and threw it toward the fence.

"Ruined, finished," he said, sitting down between the rows and holding his head in his hands.

Evelyn patted him on the shoulder and said, "We'll spray. Robert'll keep his mouth shut. Most of the plants will live."

"You're right," Blackmon said. "I'll talk to Robert."

"It's going to be a tough job," Evelyn said. "Big timber all around. Have to do some fancy flying. Might not want to do it."

"He'll do it," Blackmon said. "I heard he flew under the river bridge at Memphis last week. The FAA is looking for him. Tourists on Mud Island loved it."

Then Blackmon looked over Alligator.

"Dog's looking fit," Blackmon said. "He'll have to be to stand up to the Firecracker. Dexter's gonna lose money on this one."

"That's his business," Jack said.

"You want him to lose, don't you?" Blackmon said.

"He wants him to win," Evelyn said. "Why would he be helping with the training?"

"I heard about the training," Blackmon said. "Always thought Dumas was a good trainer. But it's not going to be a swimming race."

Jack said, "You train your dog any way you want."

"I guess Dexter knows what he's doing," Blackmon said. "Just remember I know all the tricks. Cheating is the only way I can figure Dexter won some of the fights against my dogs."

"Go tell Dexter that," Jack said. "See what he says."

Evelyn smiled, and immediately Jack was angry with himself for defending Dexter.

"The Firecracker will do my talking," Blackmon said.

Jack and Evelyn returned to town while Blackmon went to find Robert Red.

"I won't tell Dexter about the girl," Evelyn said when she got out of the truck in front of the courthouse. "Do you want him to know?"

"Probably already knows," Jack said.

Alligator yawned from the back of the truck. Jack knew Dexter was probably worried about his dog. Alligator should have been placed on his cable and fed by now.

It was growing dark, chimney swifts sailing in tight circles like bits of black paper around the courthouse chimney and the sparrows noisily going to roost in the mulberry tree by the soldier.

"I've got to get what he cares most about home," Jack said.

Evelyn smiled and said, "He cares about me."

"I wish I knew how he does it," Jack said. "Don't matter how old or how young. They all believe every word he says."

Evelyn started to speak but stopped. She looked old under the streetlight, the purple light from the mercury-vapor lamp revealing the wrinkles around her eyes and loose patches of skin on her cheeks.

As Jack drove off, he said, "You don't know anything about him at all."

She receded in the rearview mirror, looking small and frail, almost childlike, under the streetlight.

In the morning Jack watched Alligator swim in the lake from his seat in Dumas's skiff. The dog's skin had been drying out from the water, so every morning Jack rubbed baby oil on his belly and worked it into his coat.

"He'll be growing webs between his toes," Dumas said, and laughed. "I'd like to see him meet up with a gator. I know who'd win."

"Is he ready for Firecracker?" Jack asked.

"Swimming is making his muscles long and smooth. Limber is what he needs to be. But we'll put him on the treadmill before the fight. Make 'em draw up some."

Alligator swam steadily, holding his head high, his mouth open wide as he gulped air. The dog belonged in the lake, would be happy burrowing down in the mud with the snapping turtles and snakes.

First they heard the sound of the plane, the engine straining as the pilot opened the throttle to climb over the trees. The red biplane made slow turns over the lake. Finally Robert Red flew low over their heads, waggling his wings.

"Crazy man," Dumas said.

Alligator did not acknowledge the existence of the plane but kept up a steady pace ten yards from the skiff. Soon they began to smell the malathion in the air, and Dumas took the dog into the boat.

"Poison'll get up in his lungs. Hurt his wind," Dumas said.

Jack watched the plane, a small black dot against the sky, shifting in and out of his vision and wished Dumas would put Alligator ashore and row them out into the river and then down to New Orleans away from Dexter and Blackmon. Amy could meet him there, and he could get a job and forget about farming and the land, maybe living in a French Quarter apartment, watching the azaleas bloom in January while Dexter and Evelyn shivered in the Delta.

Chapter Nine

Robert Red sprayed the field three more times at one-week intervals to kill new whiteflies emerging from eggs laid on the leaves. Rainfall had been good throughout June, and the plants grew several inches a day, the branches thick with thin, pointed leaves.

The resin glands swelled with cannabinoid-filled sap that was going to buy back their land. The plants would begin to flower with the coming of the longer nights of late August and September. Blackmon planned to remove the male plants before their flowers formed and produce sinsemilla from the female plants. The females would continue to flower but produce no seeds, the power of seed making transferred into raising tall colas made up of female buds.

Jack liked to visit the field and smell the plants, the warm, wet, almost suffocating stink. Often he tried to imagine what the whole island would look like if it were planted with marijuana, grown not in rows but the seeds broadcast as in no-till planting, the plants rippling in the breeze as the colas swelled under the hot sun.

Tudor and his kin guarded the plants day and night. Blackmon had become nervous about pirates making a raid on the field and stealing the crop. They had harvested some of the leaves and Blackmon constantly had arguments with Tudor about his guards being stoned.

Blackmon called a meeting at the riverboat. When Jack arrived, they were listening to Robert Red. Robert had demanded and received a large share. Norris had complained, but Blackmon had made him shut up.

"Robert has solved our distribution problem," Blackmon said.

Robert was a slender man with a moustache. He was bald on the top of his head and had let his brown hair grow out thick and curly on the sides. His father, known throughout the Delta as Bugger Red, had also been a crop duster but had been killed in a plane crash.

He told them how he had flown in marijuana from the Smoky Mountains and cocaine from Mexico for a Lebanese in Memphis named Mike Jaban. Jaban owned a string of black nightclubs and massage parlors in Memphis.

"How much will he pay?" Evelyn asked.

Robert took a drink from a pint bottle of whiskey and said, "He'll want to see the stuff first. But he's got the money."

"We're going to be rich," Wade said.

Norris said, "If we don't get caught."

"He'll want the stuff ready to go out on the street," Robert said.

"How you going to get it up there?" Evelyn asked.

"Truck it maybe," Blackmon said. "I don't know. We'll worry about that later." Then he turned to Jack. "I want you to go to Memphis with Robert and negotiate with Jaban."

"You go," Jack said.

"No, you can do it," Blackmon said. "If your daddy was in with us, he'd be going. We're looking at you to take his place."

"Go on, Jack," Wade said.

Jack was suspicious but liked the idea of taking Dexter's place. It was true that if Dexter had been with them, they would have sent him.

"You call him," Jack said to Robert. "We'll drive up to Memphis and talk."

"No, fly," Robert said. "Mike's impressed with airplanes. Got his own private strip by his house."

Robert handed the bottle to Jack, who took a drink, wondering what the ride to Memphis with Robert was going to be like but unwilling to let the others know he was afraid.

Jack drove out to Robert's grass airstrip, which ran parallel to the highway and only thirty yards away from it. He had a two-plane hangar and a tank for aviation fuel. The red biplane waited on the strip. A field green with young soybeans stretched away to a distant treeline that danced in the heat.

"High or low?" Robert Red asked.

"What?" Jack said.

"I can fly high or low," Robert said. "When I flew brass around in 'Nam, I always asked a passenger if he wanted high or low. Some wanted low. Never could understand that. Flying high's a lot safer. Sometimes we'd touch down with branches in the skids."

"High," Jack said.

"We'll fly over the field on the island," Robert said. "I want to show you something."

Jack sat in the open cockpit in front of Robert. They took off and flew over the lake. Robert circled the field, a green grid surrounded by thick timber, the tops of the big trees interlocking so they looked solid enough to walk on. Below Jack could see the plants amid the corn, the plants a brighter green with a pyramidal shape to them. The corn looked like rows of green cylinders.

A breeze blew across the field, rippling the tasseled tops of the corn. Soon ears would form, attracting raccoons that would climb the fence to eat the green ears. Blackmon did not think they would bother the marijuana. The plants would continue to grow, perhaps outstripping the corn at the end, and the females would put out their sterile flowers, raising tall colas to the sky. A bearded man walked out of the trees, shotgun in hand, and looked up at them. Jack hoped he would recognize Robert's plane.

Jack understood why Robert had flown over the field. They were going to have to find a way to conceal the shape of the plants. Perhaps they could be pruned without destroying the yield.

Robert flew high, following the river bordered by stands of

timber that grew between the levees and the brown water. Jack looked down at the huge fields on both the Mississippi and Arkansas sides, browns and tans and blacks, marked with rows of green crops. They flew through some puffy white clouds and skirted the edge of a thunderstorm.

They passed Memphis, the cluster of buildings on the bluff above the river. Jack was able to pick out the Peabody Hotel. Past the city the country was made up of gently rolling hills with houses and farms scattered across them.

Robert circled a large brick house with white columns set far back from the highway. Jack saw people looking up at them from a lawn party in progress. A striped tent had been set up in a grove of huge oaks. Guests were swimming in the pool and playing tennis. Robert landed the plane on a grass strip set in the middle of a cow pasture. Black cows grazed on the other side of a three-strand barbed-wire fence.

"It's easy to tell the plants from the corn," Robert said. "The narcotics boys fly over and we're finished."

Jack said, "It'll have to be pruned to look like corn."

A Mercedes appeared. The driver was a fat man dressed in a tennis warm-up and wearing a Nike baseball cap. His hair was cut very short in a line above his ears. He did not speak to them, only got out and opened the door. Jack saw a sawed-off shotgun on the front seat. He watched the back of the driver's big neck as they drove up to the house.

They met with Mike Jaban, who was dressed in tennis shorts, his glossy blue-black hair cut short, on an open-air patio that was air-conditioned. Clouds formed just above their heads and on the edges of the patio where the cool, dry air from the blowers met the hot, humid air. Bugs crackled as they flew into the electric bug catchers. The tennis courts were nearby, and Jack heard the pop of the rackets on the balls and the squeak of the players' shoes, the sounds heightened by the fog.

"Robert tells me you got a business proposition," Mike said. He spoke slowly and distinctly, as if he were arguing a case before a judge, his accent clipped and sharp, but beneath was a Delta voice. Jaban still dropped his *r*'s if he was not careful.

"I came to talk," Jack said.

"How much have you got?" Mike asked.

"Ten tons of sinsemilla," Jack said.

"We're doing it right," Robert said. "All our stuff will smoke good."

"I'll pay by weight and grade," Jaban said. "It has to be dried. I'm not paying for water. I want the colas dried and baled separate. I'll make you a good price on delivery."

"We're expecting two million a ton," Jack said.

Jaban laughed, a sound that reminded Jack of the bark of a dog.

"You won't get that," Jaban said. "Half a million is the best I can do."

"Million-five," Jack said. "Half up front."

Jaban turned in his chair and called into the fog, "Billy Ray, these gentlemen want to go back to their airplane."

The fat driver stepped out of the fog.

"Million and a quarter," Jack said.

Jaban said, "One. Nothing up front."

"Take it," Robert Red whispered in Jack's ear.

"You want it brought here?" Jack asked.

Jaban smiled.

"We'll set up a place when you got something to sell," Jaban said.

Robert Red watched a girl walk across one end of the patio and disappear into the fog.

Mike said, "I've got to meet with some business associates. You can swim, play tennis, eat. Billy Ray will take you to the plane."

They went inside and wandered about the big house. It seemed as if there were a Jacuzzi in every room. Robert got them drinks from a waiter. Three couples were in one big Jacuzzi, sipping drinks and watching a tape of the Super Bowl on a huge TV screen.

Robert met an unattached girl and went off with her. Jack

wandered about the house, a southern mansion decorated on the inside to look like a nomad's tent. The walls were hung with Mideastern tapestries. Thick oriental carpets covered the polished oak floor. There were flat loaves of Lebanese bread on a buffet along with meat wrapped in grape leaves.

Jack went to look for Robert, not wanting Robert to get so drunk he could not fly. Coming down the huge main staircase, he saw Mike Jaban with a girl in a summer dress. Billy Ray carried three tennis rackets. Jack saw the emerald earrings sparkle. It was Amy.

She saw him and stopped, the same expression on her face as she had that day in the yard when Alligator almost got her. Amy said something to Mike, but Jack could not hear the words. She turned and ran back up the stairs.

Mike came down the stairs.

"Women are always forgetting something," he said, and laughed.

Mike called a waiter over and got Jack a drink.

"Play tennis if you want. There's clothes in the locker room," he said. "Have a good time."

Shadowed by Billy Ray, he went out of the house.

Jack took the steps two at a time and walked down a hall. He pushed open the first door. She was sitting in front of a mirror, crying.

"Needed some new clothes?" Jack asked.

"Mike's been nice to me," she said. She wiped her eyes. "You shouldn't be here. Come see me tomorrow."

"Why should you leave all this?" he asked.

She put her arms around him and said, "What if you get shot by the cops? Where does that leave me? I had to protect myself."

"And dress well doing it," he said. He tugged at her dress. "He buy you that?"

Jack did not like being jealous over Amy. But he realized there was nothing he could do. Right then he would have welcomed Billy Ray coming through the door with Mike behind him.

"You've got to get out of here," she said. "Billy Ray—"

"I don't want you seeing Mike again," Jack found himself saying.

He would have much rather walked off and not seen her again.

"I won't," she said. "I care about you, Jack."

"Does he let Billy Ray watch?" Jack asked.

"You bastard," she said.

She took a swing at him, but he caught her hand, fighting the impulse to hit her.

"I'm a dumb bastard all right to get mixed up with you," he said.

He walked out of the room and started down the stairs, only to meet Mike and Billy Ray coming up.

"Looking for a tennis racket," Jack said.

"Good, I need a fourth for doubles," Mike said.

Billy Ray went upstairs and returned to whisper in Mike's ear. Then Mike went upstairs. Billy Ray took Jack to the locker room and found him a racket.

They went to wait for Mike on the court. Jack watched the other players warm up. They were good.

"Does Mike play like them?" Jack asked a man waiting his turn on the court.

"Better," the man said. "Mike's played some satellite tournaments in doubles. Got himself a few Grand Prix points."

Mike and Amy showed up. Jack was paired with one of the other men. Mike showed off as he warmed up. He hit volleys behind his back and shots between his legs. A crowd had gathered, and they applauded and laughed. Jack tried to meet the ball and get it over the net. He had played some in high school, but he knew these men could play like professionals.

Jack's partner, Lawrence, positioned him between the alley lines.

"Just protect your alley," Lawrence said. "I'll take most of the volleys and all the overheads. Hit the ball down the middle. Don't try anything fancy."

Jack and Lawrence won the toss and Lawrence served. The first time Mike had a chance at an overhead he went through Jack at the net. The ball hit him on the thigh.

"Sorry," Mike said.

Women in the crowd giggled. Amy sat in a folding chair outside the fence and pouted.

When Jack received serve, Mike served Jack wide and low, running him into the fence. The crowd laughed. The next time the ball bounced high and away from him almost at a right angle. At forty-love he was ready for the funny bounce, but this time Mike made the ball hop in the opposite direction, and he was left swinging at air.

Billy Ray laughed so hard he spilled his beer on the woman standing next to him.

Mike hit Jack with five consecutive overheads. He had moved up from the legs and was aiming for the head. Mike smiled and said he was sorry after each one. The crowd continued to laugh, but when Jack moved his head as Mike swung and felt the wind from the ball on his cheek, they were silent. Only Billy Ray laughed.

Finally Mike hit a short lob over Jack's alley. Lawrence yelled, "Mine," and moved over to take it, but Jack ignored him, shouldering the little man aside. He saw Mike smiling at him at the net, confident he could pick off the smash. Jack swung hard at the ball, catching it in the center of the racket and popping his wrist. There was a solid sound as the ball caught Mike in the throat, and the man went down. The crowd gasped and was silent. Mike lay choking on the ground.

"Swallowed his tongue," Lawrence said.

Lawrence jumped the net. He reached down Jaban's throat and, hooking a finger around the tongue, pulled it out. Mike got his breath back, coughing and spitting.

"Sorry," Jack said. "We still got a deal?"

"Yeah," Mike said. He turned to Billy Ray and said, "Get them out of here."

* * *

Jack found Robert Red in a Jacuzzi with two girls. A piece of white cloth with golden threads woven into it was stretched over the tub, making it look as if they were inside a tent. The girls and Robert tried to get him into the tub, but Jack refused.

"Can you fly?" Jack asked as he pulled Robert out of the tub.

"I'm careful now," Robert said. "Drinking and flying was what did Bugger in. Flew into some power lines near our house and got his tail caught. Instead of panicking he gave it full throttle and tried to pull away. Line stretched like a big rubber band instead of breaking." Robert dried himself with a towel and pulled on his pants. "I was playing Indians with Jimmy Sikes. Didn't know what the sound was when his fuel tank exploded. We could see the smoke."

Billy Ray drove them to the plane.

"Who was that pretty girl Mike was with?" Robert asked Billy Ray.

Robert sat up so Billy Ray could see him in the rearview mirror.

"She's got green eyes and was wearing green earrings," Robert said. "She smiles like this."

Robert gave Billy Ray a smile in the mirror that looked like the expression of a man who had just stepped on a snake.

"You know her?" Robert asked. "I want her phone number."

Jack gave Robert a poke in the ribs with his elbow.

"Leave him alone," Jack whispered.

"Me and Billy Ray are pals," Robert said. "Ain't that right, Billy Ray?"

Billy Ray kept both hands on the wheel and his eyes fixed straight ahead. Jack hoped he would not start looking at the sawed-off shotgun.

"You been slipping out with her?" Robert asked. "Been in the hot tub?" Robert laughed. "Hell, Billy Ray, you wouldn't fit in half those tubs."

Billy Ray made an animallike sound deep in his throat. Jack watched his right hand carefully in case he made a move for the shotgun.

"Shut up," Jack said to Robert.

Robert said, "Cat got your tongue, Billy Ray?"

Billy Ray hit the brakes hard. Jack caught himself, but Robert was thrown against the front seat.

The back of Billy Ray's neck was red, the veins standing out.

"Out," Billy Ray said, not bothering to turn around.

His hand was on the shotgun.

Jack opened the door and pulled Robert out of the car. They were close to the airstrip. Fat black cows stared at them from across a fence. Billy Ray drove off, leaving them standing in a cloud of dust.

"Guess he don't like me," Robert said.

They got in the plane, and Jack felt better as he watched Robert Red go through his preflight check: gunning the engine, reading dials, and working the controls. The takeoff was a smooth one, but he became uneasy when Robert Red buzzed the house, flying so low the guests on the lawn ducked. He saw Amy standing with Mike and Billy Ray on the front porch. She lifted her head to watch, her face a pale spot next to Mike's dark one.

Then Robert Red headed for home. Instead of flying high, he flew low, skimming the tops of the trees. When they reached the river, he got down low on the water. They missed a towboat by only a few feet, the pilot blowing his horn at them. Soon Memphis came up, the bluff rising high above them on the left.

They flew between the pilings for the new river bridge, and Jack saw the steamboats used to carry tourists on the river moored in the harbor at Mud Island. As they came up on the highway and railroad bridges, built side by side, Jack tried to gauge how much margin for error Robert Red had. It did not look like much.

A few hundred yards from the bridge Robert Red rolled the plane and things became all jumbled up for Jack. They flew under, the engine roaring at full throttle, and he saw brown water and blue sky and the spidery frames of the bridges. Gravity pulled his body tight against the straps of the harness. The wind sang through the struts. Then they were clear, Robert putting the plane into a steep climb.

Jack felt sick. Putting his head between his legs he threw up. He smelled the sour stink and thought of Alligator.

Robert followed the river the rest of the way home. He made a perfect landing, and as Jack climbed out of the plane, he decided he was going to give Robert the beating he deserved.

"Goddamn, that's something to tell your grandbabies about," Robert Red said. "Even old Bugger never did that. Hey, let's do it again!"

Instead of hitting him Jack laughed.

"Not with me," Jack said.

Jack realized it was Mike Jaban's face he wanted to smash. Amy had not looked too upset when Jaban was down on the court choking to death. Maybe it was just business to her. He remembered what she had said about not being able to love anyone. She knew herself, but he did not. Was he just like Dexter, doomed to search for love among hookers and mistresses?

I won't be like him, Jack thought. I'm not one of his dogs.

This time he had gotten the better of Dexter. Blackmon and the others were beginning to look to him instead of the old man. When the money came in, Dexter would be left out, finished.

But Jack thought of Alligator, who could do nothing but fight, his every move determined by generations of fighting dogs before him. He was trapped just as surely as the dog, the old man sitting at home with a grin on his face, waiting for the sureness of the blood.

Chapter Ten

J ack, along with the whole community, black and white, turned out early one Sunday morning to prune the plants. The sun came up as they crossed the mist-covered lake. Jack pulled his baseball cap down low over his eyes against the glare. He dreaded the taste of dust in his mouth, the sweat puddling on his body to be slowly evaporated by the sun, a salty crust remaining behind.

Sally Ann, who taught second grade at the private school, and Lucinda Williams, who taught at the public school, organized the children into squads and used posters and a sample plant to show them how to prune the lower branches.

"Now what do you cut, children?" Lucinda asked, a tall black woman dressed in a pair of nylon jogging shorts and a tank top.

"The tips," they replied.

"And how do you measure?" Sally Ann asked. "Where are your little rulers?"

They held up strips of construction paper.

The teachers issued the children safety scissors with blunt ends and marched them off into the field.

"Aren't they cute, Jack?" Sally Ann said.

"Dammit, Sally Ann, do you think this is a church picnic?" Norris asked.

Norris had been worrying about getting caught. He called Wade three or four times a day to make sure there were no narcotics agents in the county.

The adults pruned the tops. Jack worked with Blackmon and

Travis. Tudor and his kin roamed the fields with plastic garbage bags, gathering up the branches. Tudor wore sunglasses and carried a shotgun slung over his shoulder with a strap made out of a piece of yellow ski rope. He smoked a misshapen joint the size of a cigar.

"Tudor, I told you to quit smoking that stuff," Blackmon said.

Tudor laughed and said, "I'm used to it. Nothing more to me than a good chew."

"That stuff you're collecting belongs to all of us," Blackmon said. "I don't want to see it grow legs and walk off."

Wade appeared out of the plants.

"I've been watching him," Wade said. "Won't be sneaking off."

"You better watch everybody," Tudor said. "Folks are chopping off dollar bills."

Tudor disappeared into the plants, carrying his plastic bag and leaving a trail of bluish smoke.

"Hot day," Blackmon said.

"We're putting in air-conditioning at the school with our money," Travis said.

"That's real fine," Blackmon said.

Travis said, "School board's been trying to get that done for five years."

Blackmon and his friends still controlled the school board.

"No money," Blackmon said.

"You got the private school air-conditioned," Travis said.

"Think about that word 'private,' " Blackmon said.

"Why don't you leave the running of the schools to us?" Travis asked.

"Because we pay the taxes," Blackmon said.

Both men had stopped pruning and stood looking at each other.

"Save your arguing for the board meeting," Evelyn said as she stepped into their row. "Do you want to start a fight and stop the work?"

"He wants to keep us down," Travis said.

"Try working," Blackmon said.

"You got all the land," Travis said.

"Be quiet," Evelyn said.

The people in the rows around them had stopped working and were listening, waiting.

"Nobody will get anything if we don't get these plants pruned," Evelyn said in a whisper.

"Show me how you're pruning so fast," Blackmon said to Travis.

"You're not using those shears right," Travis said.

Around them, hidden by the plants, Jack began to hear the click of shears and the soft murmur of voices, black and white.

Robert Red flew over several times to check on the work and told them over the radio that the plants they had pruned looked much like the corn.

They broke for lunch. The women had brought enough food for a battalion: fried chicken, potato salad, chili, fried tomatoes, and homemade bread. They ate off the cotton wagons pulled up under the shade of the big cottonwood. Tudor and his kin hung the prunings on pieces of string to dry in the sun.

"Where's Bascomb Dodd?" Jack asked Blackmon.

"Holding church," Blackmon said. "Only people there are old folks too feeble to come out here. Probably preaching hellfire against us."

"Did you invite him?" Jack asked.

Evelyn walked up.

"Me and Evelyn did," Blackmon said.

"Bascomb said he didn't hold with working on the Sabbath," Evelyn said.

Blackmon said, "He sure won't be turning down his share of the profits."

"He doesn't matter," Evelyn said.

"That's easy for you to say," Blackmon said. "You go to that Episcopal church in Greenville. I got to sit in church on Wednesday night and look him in the eye."

"Don't go," Jack said.

They both gave him a hard stare.

"It's not that easy," Blackmon said. "Church is my only chance of not going to hell."

Jack laughed.

"He's just like his daddy," Blackmon said. "A damn atheist."

Jack said, "I'm not like him."

Evelyn and Blackmon laughed.

"You remind me more of Dexter every day," Evelyn said.

Jack wondered if Blackmon knew about Dexter and Evelyn and thought about saying something to her. But he found it difficult to attack people he had been saying "Yes, sir" and "Yes, ma'am" to all his life. So he turned his back to them and walked off.

After lunch the children took naps. They never got the younger ones back out in the field again. Sally Ann and Lucinda spent their time breaking up fights and comforting children who wanted their mothers.

All afternoon the clouds built up over the river, at first a light grey but later changing to black. The wind began to blow in strong gusts, kicking up clouds of dust and bending the plants and corn. Jack and a few others took refuge under the cotton wagons. Then the rain came, sounding as if the deer herd were running through the dry leaves toward them. Jack could barely see the field through the rain, the plants tossed by the wind and looking dim and ghostlike in the flashes of lightning.

Everyone was quiet during the worst of the storm, the children clinging to their mothers. Blackmon traced patterns with his finger in the powder-fine dust. Then the storm moved off, and the rain let up some. People began to talk.

"What you gonna do when you get rich?" a man asked Wade.

"Buy me a houseboat and take a year going down to New Orleans," Wade said.

"I'm putting a new kitchen in the Gulf Shores house," Sally Ann said. "I got that from Daddy. Norris hasn't gotten around to losing it yet."

"We should have invested the money you wasted on that house," Norris said. "I told you a hundred times that—"

Sally Ann gave him a mean look and Norris shut up.

"I want one of those center-pivot irrigation systems," Evelyn said. "I'll sit on the porch and watch it roll up and down the field during an August drought."

"I want a seat on the stock exchange," Norris said.

Sally Ann said, "You'll live in New York alone."

"Aw, Sally Ann, you'll like it better than Jackson," Norris said. Everyone laughed.

"We'll buy books for the school. Scholarships for college. Air-conditioning," Travis said. "We'd do all that if we got the shares we deserve."

"You better make do with what you got," Blackmon said. "You're not getting more."

Travis started to say something to Blackmon, but Evelyn interrupted him and said, "What do you want, Jack?"

Jack wanted to say Amy, and wondered if Evelyn knew. But he also wanted their land back. He picked up a handful of dust.

"I want my land back," Jack said. "My land, not Daddy's."

Blackmon laughed.

"Dexter working for you," Blackmon said. "I'd like to see that."

The rain stopped and the clouds drifted away, leaving the field steaming under the hot sun. Jack walked into the field barefoot, feeling the wet earth squeeze up between his toes. He smelled the plants and listened to the water drip from their leaves, which had been turned a brighter shade of green by the rain. They were growing fast, the resin glands swelling, as the plants pushed upward for the sun, trying to overtake the taller corn.

By the end of the day they had pruned almost half the field. Blackmon announced they would return the next Sunday to finish the job.

Bascomb Dodd's face glowed red under the early-morning sun as he stood on a cotton wagon, the people gathered around him. A pale yellow sun slid in and out of the thin clouds, the treeline reduced to a shadowy grey line by the haze. The wet heavy air made it difficult to breathe. It had been too hot to sleep the night before. Jack had lain naked on the sheets and sweated, the fan in the window blowing his own and Alligator's stink about the room.

"This time we're going to keep the Sabbath," Bascomb said.

Jack imagined Bascomb was going to preach a short sermon.

"We will build a church here, a bush arbor," Bascomb said. "We will worship the Lord at noon."

The older people became excited. Jack did not even know what a bush arbor was.

"I helped build them when I was a boy," Blackmon said. "There'd be some mighty fine preaching under them."

They set posts in the ground and built a framework of saplings higher than a man's head. Then they cut down small trees, mostly sweet gums, and piled them on the frame. It was shady under the arbor, but nothing could make it cool. Jack smelled the sap that oozed out of the cut wood, and the scent of crushed leaves filled the air.

Then they set to work pruning the remaining plants. Robert Red and Wade worked with Jack.

"Norris is right," Wade said. "If just one narcotics enforcement plane makes a pass over this field, we're finished."

"No, it won't look that different from the corn," Robert said. "Most of 'em will be flying high. They don't have time to fly the whole Delta that low. They're looking for shapes. We'll fool 'em."

"He's right," Jack said.

"Has anyone been snooping around?" Robert asked.

Wade said, "No, but they will. They'll be on this field like flies on a rotten watermelon."

"Blackmon'll take care of them," Robert said. "Those catfishermen pull guard duty."

"Maybe, but I don't believe everyone's kept their mouth shut," Wade said.

They worked all morning. Dodd stayed under the arbor making notes for the sermon he was going to preach before the noon meal. Evelyn and Travis directed the barbecuing of pigs in open pits. Then they gathered beneath the arbor. Jack shared a jug of ice water with Robert Red. Dodd put on his jacket and stepped up on a low stage made by placing boards across a frame of coolers.

"I thought I had experienced the joy of God," Bascomb said. "I thought I had tasted the sweetness. But I was wrong."

Bascomb paused and let the words sink in. Jack wished he had stayed away. He smelled their sweat. The scent of barbecue was in the air. A mosquito buzzed in his ear.

Dodd held a marijuana branch above his head.

"God is in these leaves," he said. "The sweetness is here."

A murmur ran through the crowd.

"Old fool has gone crazy," Robert whispered to Jack.

"Drinking takes you away from God. Dancing takes you away. Fornicating takes you away. This weed is God. It is love."

"Those catfishermen must be walking through the pearly gates," Blackmon said. "They've smoked enough of it."

The splotches on Dodd's face glowed red.

"Earl, you have always been a mocker," Dodd said. "The fiery pit waits for you."

"Can't be any hotter than it is today," Blackmon said.

No one laughed. Blackmon left the arbor.

"We all move too fast," Dodd continued. "We run to Kmart and buy color TVs and records. Satan is the one who's celebrated, not God. We are frozen in a moment of love that is like God's eternal love, timeless, without end. When we sell it, we're sending out God to America. We will build us a great church. But beware. All is corrupted by music that stirs the passions and keeps us from loving God."

Jack agreed with Robert. Bascomb had gone crazy. But the crowd did not think so. They were silent as if waiting for him to reveal some great truth.

"I have the proof," Bascomb said.

He stepped down from the platform and opened one of the coolers. The smell of cornbread filled the arbor.

"Smoking it is wrong," Bascomb continued as he pulled a wedge of cornbread out of the cooler. "Take this, eat. Let the children eat too."

Bascomb handed the wedge to Mr. Francis the storekeeper, who hesitated, then took a bite out of it. The crowd watched to see what was going to happen.

Francis grinned and said, "Nothing to it."

Then he ate the rest of it as Bascomb and some of the men handed out the rest of the pieces.

"You will feel God's love as I have," Bascomb shouted over the buzz of the crowd.

The bread came around to Jack. He and Robert ate.

For a while Jack felt nothing. Then the world slowed down. He watched a leaf quiver in the top of a cottonwood while the liquid thonk, thonk, thonk of a rain crow, calling from deep in the woods, vibrated through his body. Out in the field he watched the tops of the plants swaying in the breeze, keeping time with the beating of his heart.

As the crowd passed around the cornbread, Bascomb climbed back up on his stage.

"Let the love of God flow into you," Bascomb said.

In response someone giggled.

"I'm hungry," a child said.

The crowd laughed.

"Those pigs should be about done," Wade said.

The crowd started to drift out of the arbor.

"Together we will feel his love," Bascomb said. "Do not be led into gluttony."

But they paid no attention to him.

"I am fucked up," Robert Red said.

Jack and Robert followed the crowd.

"Come back!" Bascomb shouted. "Do not be led into the way of the devil! He will use your senses to corrupt you."

The crowd pulled the pigs out of the pit and quickly stripped them to the bones. Jack stuffed the meat into his mouth, licking the sauce off his fingers. Two children were using their fingers to clean out a jar of peanut butter. Bascomb wandered among them, preaching doom for all.

Blackmon and the catfishermen continued to work on the plants. Evelyn too had refused to eat and stood with arms folded watching the people and shaking her head at their antics.

Someone suggested they swim in the river to cool off. Some went through the trees, but Jack followed a dirt track. The woods were crawling with snakes, and Evelyn might not be around the next time.

Jack walked out of the trees onto the gleaming white sandbar. Norris and Sally Ann were swimming naked in the river. Sally Ann was built better than Jack had thought. Children played in a shallow eddy at one end of the sandbar watched over by Wade, who had taken off his shirt and rolled up his jeans. Tudor and his kin, marked by a cloud of bluish smoke, crept up through a canebrake to watch the swimmers. Jack wished Amy were with him, that he were swimming with her. Then he was angry at himself for thinking of her and pushed her out of his mind.

Bascomb came out of the trees wearing his coat but nothing else. The sweat glistened on his face.

"Take off your coat and come on in, Brother Bascomb," Robert Red yelled at him. "Never enjoyed church so much."

Bascomb stopped and surveyed the scene on the sandbar. He had a smile on his face, his balls loose and his cock dangling.

"God is love," Jack said, pointing to the naked swimmers.

"My church, my church," Bascomb muttered as he walked down to the water.

Jack sat in the shade of a clump of willows until the sun, which he did not think was ever going to move, was low over the trees on the Arkansas shore. He watched the people and a cypress snag slowly bobbing in the current. Finally the snag began to move in real time, a quick, jerky motion. The people left the water and, after shaking sand from their clothes and dressing, wandered off into the trees. Norris and Sally Ann still swam in the river, floating about on a piece of driftwood.

The evening star had come up above the river when Evelyn and Blackmon walked down from the trees and sat next to him.

"Pruning's done," Blackmon said. He watched a couple dressed in their underwear throwing a Frisbee. "Wonder what church with Brother Bascomb will be like next Sunday?"

Evelyn laughed.

"As long as he serves cornbread he'll pack the place," she said.

Blackmon walked over to talk to Norris and Sally Ann.

"You better get out before the mosquitoes carry you off," Blackmon yelled.

Norris and Sally Ann waved to him and laughed.

"Looks like we're going to make a crop," Jack said.

"Dexter didn't believe we could do it," Evelyn said.

"He doesn't know everything."

"It's not made yet."

"Do you want it to fail so he'll be right?" Jack asked.

"No."

Norris came out of the water for Sally Ann's clothes. He and Blackmon turned their backs while she dressed.

"I guess all this is worth getting our land back," Evelyn said.

"Dexter thinks he'll do it with Alligator," Jack said.

Evelyn said, "He might."

"No, he's just as wrong as Bascomb Dodd thinking he could found a church on dope," Jack said.

"Don't be so hard on Dexter," Evelyn said.

"Why don't you marry him?" Jack said.

"He hasn't asked," she said.

"When we sell the plants, he'll have nothing. I'll have land," Jack said.

"Try to understand him," Evelyn said.

"Oh, I do," Jack said. "He wants everything his own way. Don't you care about all his women?"

She pushed a hole in the sand with the toe of her boot, the sand squeaking under the pressure.

"I care about him," Evelyn said.

Blackmon along with Sally Ann and Norris walked up.

"I'll have an apartment in Manhattan," Norris said.

"I'll put in a microwave at Gulf Shores. And one of those refrigerators with ice water in the door," Sally Ann said.

Blackmon laughed and said, "That crop ain't made yet."

They walked off the sandbar. A towboat coming down from Memphis blew its horn and then it was quiet again, the river making a hissing sound as it swept past the curve of the sandbar. All the stars were out. They entered the insect-loud trees.

"We'll fly to Paris for my clothes," Sally Ann said.

Jack thought of Dexter in bed with Amy and felt rage against his father. He drove his fist into his hand.

Evelyn touched his arm.

"Talk to him," she said.

Jack pushed her hand away and walked away from them. He smelled the field before he saw it, the scent of the prunings heavy in the air.

Selling the plants, buying back the land, was all that was important, he told himself. With the money he could have a dozen Amys. But then he saw her taking an earring in and out of her ear, the stones flashing green in the light, and felt a deep ache within him just as insistent as the flow of the river toward the sea.

Chapter Eleven

Jack threw clay pigeons for Evelyn from the shade of the porch. He did not use a hand trap but tossed the targets backhanded like a man throwing a Frisbee, sending them sailing across the lawn in slow, high arcs. She waited until the pigeon paused at the top of the arc and then squeezed the trigger. He watched her break twenty-five straight. Alligator lay stretched out on his side in front of a fan at one end of the porch, his chain hooked to a heavy eyebolt set in the rail.

"Dexter's gone to Greenville," Jack said.

"I know," she said.

Jack could not understand why she allowed Dexter to make a fool of her. She did not seem to care how many women he had been with or what he had done to her friend Margaret.

"Wonder what he's doing?" he asked.

"Pull," she said.

He threw the pigeon low and hard. She shot and missed.

She placed the pistol on the porch rail and said, "None of my business where he goes."

"He may be fooling you," Jack said. "But he can't fool me."

"Talk to him," Evelyn said. "He cared about Margaret."

"Don't talk about her," Jack said.

"A good-looking man could always make Margaret's eyes light up," Evelyn said. "Didn't you know that?"

"Did he tell you that?"

"No, I knew it. Everybody knew."

"He's the one who started that story. He could make her believe she was crazy. He could make her do or believe anything because she loved him."

Alligator got up and shook his head, rattling the chain. He turned around several times and lay back down.

"She left because of his women," Jack said. "Has he convinced you they didn't exist?"

"Their marriage was a mistake. Wasn't all Dexter's fault," she said.

"He's probably with some whore in Greenville right now," Jack said, but was immediately sorry he had said it.

Evelyn picked up the pistol and said, "Throw me another low one."

Jack threw the pigeon hard and low. She shot almost as soon as it left his hand, and the pigeon vanished in a puff of black smoke.

"You are a damn fool," Evelyn said.

Before Jack could answer, he heard a car lock its brakes out on the road and looked up to watch a yellow car slide past the driveway. It was Amy. She backed up and drove toward the house, gravel spraying beneath the tires.

"It's Mary Ann," Evelyn said.

"Her name's Amy," Jack said.

"Why, she told me it was Mary Ann," Evelyn said.

"Can't help lying," Jack said. "Second nature to her."

Evelyn gave him a jab in the ribs and said, "You hush up about her."

Amy, dressed in tennis shorts, got out of the car and ran up the steps. Her eyes were red. But she had a determined look on her face as if she planned to do no more crying. She straightened her hair as she came up the steps, the emerald earrings flashing.

"I'm on my way to New Orleans," Amy said.

Evelyn said, "I was just going to get us a beer."

She went inside, the screen door slamming behind her.

"Billy Ray's going to kill me," Amy said in a flat, even voice.

"Mike caught you messing around?" Jack said.

She bit her lip and pouted. He wished he had not said it.

"I need a place to stay," she said. "But not here. Where's Dexter?"

"In Greenville with some hooker," Jack said, waiting for a reaction, but she stood there and looked him in the eye, her teeth clenched tightly. "Why not go to New Orleans?"

He could feel the tug of her on him as if he were tied to her with a stronger chain than Alligator's.

"They'll find me," she said.

Evelyn returned with the beer.

"Mary Ann, New Orleans is my favorite city," Evelyn said. "My husband and I used to go down for the Ole Miss–Tulane game. We stayed at the Roosevelt Hotel."

"Mary Ann has changed her mind," Jack said. "She's staying here."

Amy gave a little jump. Evelyn smiled.

Jack said, "I'm going to show her the riverboat."

Jack loaded Alligator into the car and drove out to the riverboat. Alligator sat in the back seat and panted with his tongue hanging out. Soon his stink filled up the car.

"Don't you ever give that dog a bath?" Amy asked.

"We swim him in the lake every day," Jack said.

Amy turned off the air-conditioning and opened the windows. Soon they were sweating, Jack's shirt sticking to his back. They crossed the levee and went down toward the lake. The patches of backwater had all dried up, the mud cracked in crazy patterns. Blackmon had already begun talking about irrigating the plants.

"I can stay on the boat?" Amy asked.

"Not unless you want to pass the time of day talking to Daddy," Jack said.

Amy got out of the car and walked onto the dock.

"There's nothing out here," she said.

"Billy Ray won't find you," Jack said.

"It's hot. Just water and mud."

"You should have thought of that when you got mixed up with Mike Jaban."

She stamped her foot on the cypress boards.

"I'm going to New Orleans," she said.

Jack wished he had kept his mouth shut.

"No, you're staying here," he said.

"Where?"

"On the other side of the lake. Where Billy Ray will never find you."

"Live in the woods?"

"No, there's a place for you to stay. You'll see."

They took a johnboat across the lake, the afternoon sun shining directly in their faces. A hot breeze had brought up small whitecaps, and the boat slammed into the swells. Amy sat beside him and used her hand to shade her eyes while he ran the motor. Alligator panted in the bow. Jack worried about him getting overheated. When they reached the shade of the shoreline willows, he let Alligator go over the side to cool off. The dog swam about, sniffing at the snags and logs where turtles and snakes liked to sun themselves.

"Did he really send Billy Ray after you?" Jack asked.

"Billy Ray's been watching me," she said.

"You're good at making up stories."

"Don't you believe me?"

"Just like I did when you said you loved me."

"I do. I got bored sitting in that apartment and going to school."

"Billy Ray'll make sure you don't get bored now."

"You said nice things to me. I liked that."

Amy watched Alligator swim toward them.

She said, "You were really just getting even with Dexter."

Alligator wanted back in the boat. Jack got up and pulled him in. The dog went to the bow and shook himself.

"I told you how I felt," he said. "The old man had nothing to do with it."

Jack wished she had not stopped, had gone on to New Orleans or to California. But then the thought of not seeing her again made him afraid.

"You told me you cared," she said.

Alligator had finished licking himself off and was watching them. Some animal moved in the trees, rustling the leaves, and the dog turned his head.

"I've already told you how I feel," he said.

"Say it," she said.

Jack was not sure what to do. She was the one who claimed she loved him yet kept turning tricks. But she had come looking for him. He did not believe her story that Billy Ray was out to kill her. Pimps beat up girls and sometimes killed them. Mike Jaban was no pimp.

"You have my heart," he said.

"You're so sweet to me," she said. "I want to stay with you. Help you farm. Learn to drive a tractor."

"First, we need land."

"You'll have plenty of money from the grass."

"Crop's not made yet."

He was glad she had come, because if she had stayed in Memphis, she would have been sure to talk about the marijuana in some bar. Maybe that was why Jaban was mad at her. But he wondered if Amy would ever be able to live in the Delta. He started the motor and headed for Dumas's barge.

Jack lifted Alligator up to Dumas and then helped Amy climb on board. While Carrie showed Amy the barge, Jack explained to Dumas that Amy needed a place to hide out. Jack hoped Amy would behave herself and not refuse to stay.

But she got along with Carrie, and she did not seem bothered by the snakes. She even watched Dumas milk a big rattler. Near evening, as Jack and Dumas were preparing to swim Alligator in the lake, Amy decided she wanted to go.

"I thought you didn't like to be around Alligator," Jack said.

"I want to be with you," Amy said.

I'm a fool, Jack thought. If the old man knew he would bust a gut laughing. His little cast-off whore running me around.

But then he thought of her leaving or Billy Ray catching up with her and knew he loved her. The old man had been careful to fall in love with none of them. He might quote poetry to Evelyn, but Jack did not believe he loved even her.

Out on the lake it was still hot. The breeze had died and the dark water lay still under a cloudless sky. Jack worked the oars and watched Alligator swim. Dumas and Amy sat together on a seat. Dumas explained to her how he was conditioning Alligator for the big fight.

"I'm hot," Amy said.

"It'll be cooler soon," Dumas said.

"I'm going to swim," Amy said.

She took off her tennis shoes and socks.

"Dumas, cover your eyes," she said.

Dumas looked as if he had stepped into a pit full of rattlesnakes. He put his hands over his eyes.

"You can swim fine in those shorts," Dumas said.

"There's snakes in this lake," Jack said.

"I'm not afraid of snakes," Amy said. "Just keep that dog away from me."

She slipped out of her clothes and went over the side. Alligator ignored her as she swam a powerful crawl by the side of the boat, her white body trailing streams of bubbles through the dark water. Dumas took his hands away from his eyes, but after taking one look at the clothes on the seat beside him, he turned around and faced Jack. Jack expected her to quickly tire from the crawl, but she continued to swim at a much faster pace than Alligator. Soon she pulled ahead of the boat, and Dumas turned around to face Alligator.

When Alligator finished his swim, she was far ahead of them. They took the dog into the boat and Jack rowed fast to catch up with her. She turned and waited for them, treading water. Alligator stood in the bow with his ears raised and watched her.

"You mind that dog," she said.

Jack reached for his collar. Dumas still sat with his hands over his eyes. But he was too late. Alligator hit the water and swam straight for her. When he was an arm's length away, he turned and swam in a tight circle around her.

"Dumas, help me get Alligator back in the boat," Jack said.

But Dumas refused to uncover his eyes.

"Get him away from me," Amy said.

Jack was afraid she might start screaming, causing Alligator to get excited and latch on to her. He would not be able to hold on in the water, but one bite could easily break bones.

Amy splashed water at Alligator as he circled closer.

"Leave him alone," Jack said. "Swim to the boat."

She waited for an opening and swam for the boat with a frantic, awkward crawl. He helped her in. Alligator circled the boat while she was putting on her clothes.

"Now you can open your damn eyes," Jack said to Dumas.

"At least he's a gentleman," Amy said. "I saw you gawking at me."

Dumas pulled Alligator into the boat.

"God, he stinks," Amy said.

Alligator shook himself, spraying them all with water.

"He smells like he should," Dumas said.

"No need to worry," Jack said to Amy. "I think he likes you."

Amy said, "Keep him away from me."

"Least you ain't scared of serpents," Dumas said. "Never seen anybody take to snakes quicker."

"They're clean," Amy said.

"So is Alligator," Jack said.

Dumas took the oars for the trip back and Alligator sat at his feet.

Jack reached for Amy's hand but she pushed his away.

"Leave me alone," she said.

"What's the matter?" he asked.

"You were going to let him bite me."

"No, he surprised me. I don't think he was going to bite you. He was just curious."

She took his hand.

"Billy Ray won't come out here?"

"No," Jack said, still wondering if the threat of Billy Ray was a story she had made up.

The sun dropped behind the trees, and the lake grew dark. Jack saw some big birds, geese or cranes, flying very high in the full sunlight, the light shining off their white feathers. Dumas and Amy looked but could not see them. Then Jack lost them too.

Carrie was waiting supper for them when they got back to the barge. She had started the generator and turned on a string of different colored light bulbs at one end of the barge so it looked as if they were approaching a floating carnival. They ate fried okra, greens, and catfish. Amy cleaned her plate, asked for seconds, and drank off the pot liquor.

"Child, you'll grow as big as a house if you ain't careful," Carrie said.

"Got to keep up her strength," Dumas said. "She can outswim any fish in the lake."

After supper they sat on a screen porch Dumas had built on one end of the barge. Lightning bugs flashed in the trees. Bats twisted low over the barge in pursuit of insects attracted by the light. Whippoorwills began to call.

"Amy can help with the serpents," Dumas said.

"This girl ain't gonna be studying no snakes," Carrie said.

"I want to," Amy said.

"He'll have you out hunting in the bushes for them," Carrie said.

Amy looked into the dark trees.

"I'm not afraid," Amy said.

"You help Carrie with the cooking," Jack said.

Amy said, "I'll do what I want."

"Be careful, Dumas," Jack said. "She's going to get you snake-bit."

Dumas laughed.

"I'll teach her right," Dumas said.

They all sat for a long time in silence. Jack smelled Alligator and then saw him standing just outside the porch watching them.

"I wish you'd keep him chained up," Carrie said.

"He won't bother nobody," Dumas said.

"Come on, old man," Carrie said. "Come help me fix up Luther's room for Amy."

Amy sat and looked hard at the dog.

"I can't stare him down," she said.

"I should leave him here," Jack said. "Just in case Billy Ray makes it out here."

"I thought you said he wouldn't," she said.

"Not a chance."

"I don't want that dog here."

"Don't worry. He's not staying."

"How do these people live out here all alone?"

"Stay busy."

"Do you think they love each other?"

"Sure."

"Jack, I want to learn to love you. I went with Mike because I was scared of loving you."

"Don't talk about that."

"I won't let you down this time."

Jack thought of Dexter laughing at him.

Amy said, "Stay with me tonight."

"I can't. Daddy will come looking for Alligator. He'll think something's gone wrong with the training."

"You come back tomorrow?"

"I bring the dog out here every day."

"Get rid of him."

"I like to train him. Gives me an edge on the old man."

"Dexter is making a fool out of you."

Jack realized he was going to stay with her.

"I'll stay," he said. "But the old man will probably have break-fast with us in the morning."

"I don't care what he does," she said. "Please stay."

"I want to stay. Because of you."

"That's sweet. Nobody has ever been sweet to me like you."

She threw her arms around his neck. Startled by the sudden movement, Alligator raised his ears.

"Chain him up. Please," she said.

So Jack put Alligator on his chain, and they went to bed in Luther's room, the walls covered with posters of professional football players.

She traced the scars on his chest with her fingertips.

"Do they hurt?" she asked.

"They itch sometimes," he said.

She kissed his scars and took him in her mouth.

Jack lay back and looked up at a poster on the ceiling of a running back breaking into the clear. She still smelled of the lake, and he had Alligator's scent on him.

Alligator's chain rattled. There was a high-pitched squeal. Alligator began to shake something. Amy sat upright.

"What's that?"

"Coons trying to raid Carrie's garden. I chained Alligator up next to it. He got one."

Jack reached up and pulled her down onto the bed, hoping to lose himself in her. But it was no use. It was as if Dexter were in the room, watching with a leer on his face.

"Don't you like me?" she asked.

Then he got mad at her and at the old man.

"You're so big," she whispered in his ear.

He felt as if he were diving to the bottom of the lake to touch the ribs of the old sidewheeler whose boiler had exploded and that had sunk in the channel. The grinning face of the old man disappeared. Then she went to sleep or pretended to, and he continued searching with her for that place where none of them could touch him, where there was no Dexter or Mike Jaban or fighting dogs.

Chapter Twelve

J ack felt the weight of the Airlight .38 on his belt as he walked
with Blackmon along the dirt track. Tudor had discovered
someone had been watching the field. Tonight they had set an
ambush for them. He watched the darkness, waiting for some
shape to take form out of it, no longer worrying about stepping on
a snake. The dust was powder fine beneath his feet. The cicadas
made a brittle whine in the trees. It was almost like going out on a
night patrol in Vietnam except then he was almost never afraid and
now the fear made his legs feel weak and unsteady just as they did
before the first hit of a football game.

"Probably just poaching deer," Jack said.

"No, they're after the crop," Blackmon said. "We've got to
make an example of them."

"By doing what?"

"Have to catch them first."

They reached the field, and Jack heard the clatter of the gear on
the sprinkler nozzles and the hum of generators. Blackmon had
run lines to the river and was pumping water out of it. Now Tudor
and his kin had generators and sprinklers to tend in addition to
guarding the plants. Three sprinklers squirted streams of water in
fifty-yard circles. The plants smelled fresh, the air cooler. The
cicadas whined with a deeper hum. In a few weeks they would
begin removing the male plants before they released their pollen.
Then the females would form sinsemilla, the plants continuing to
flower and raising huge colas covered with resin glands.

Tudor met them at the big cottonwood. He had one of the

walkie-talkies that belonged to the sheriff's office. Jack was glad it was dark so he would not have to look into Tudor's little black eyes or at the skin that was always pale white even in the middle of the summer. And Tudor smelled like fish.

"They've landed below the big sandbar," Tudor said. "Lonnie saw 'em."

They followed Tudor through the woods into the thicker darkness beneath the trees where there was not even starlight. Neither Blackmon nor Tudor used their five-cell flashlights. Jack kept walking into branches and tangling his feet in vines and briars. Blackmon stepped on a covey of quail that exploded with squeals into the night. Jack ended up on the ground with the .38 in his hand. Tudor laughed at them. Near the end of the field he stopped.

"They'll come up to this corner," Tudor whispered. "We'll wait for 'em."

"No shooting unless they shoot first," Blackmon said.

"A few booby traps in the woods would've stopped them the first time," Tudor said. "Lonnie says he can make some easy."

"No traps, no shooting," Blackmon said.

"You're the boss," Tudor said.

Blackmon said, "That's right. Don't you forget it."

They set up their ambush in a stand of cane. One of the sprinklers was close by and a breeze carried a fine mist down on them.

Jack was no longer afraid for himself. He hoped that Tudor was not going to shoot the pirates.

The pirates came through the woods making plenty of noise. One stepped on a dry twig that broke with a loud snap.

"Goddamn, be careful!" one of them said.

Then they were at the fence, two dark shapes. If it had been a real ambush, he would have shot them already.

A wire cutter made a metallic click. Blackmon stood up and turned on his flashlight, holding it away from his body.

"Don't move!" Blackmon shouted.

Jack saw their frightened young faces in the light.

"Please! Don't shoot!" one of them said, dropping an armful of plastic bags and trying to shade the light from his eyes with his hands.

"Oh, Jesus!" the other said, still holding the wire cutters.

While Blackmon held his rifle on them, Tudor searched them and found they were unarmed. One wore a cap with a chicken-plant logo. They had sharp noses and stooped shoulders. Tudor's kin gone to town.

"We just wanted some to smoke," the one with the cap said.

"That's why you brought all those plastic bags," Blackmon said, giving the bags a kick.

Lonnie came out of the trees.

"I knocked a hole in their boat," Lonnie said. "River took it."

"Good, you and Tudor take care of them," Blackmon said.

"Please, we won't tell nobody," the one with the cap said. "I'm George Carter." He motioned to the other man. "This is Thomas Tate. We're good Mississippi boys. I'm kin to all the Hollandale Carters."

The man pointed off into the darkness as if he wanted to convince them he knew the way to Hollandale.

George continued, "We won't ever come back."

"We won't tell nobody," Thomas said.

"Now we just can't take that chance," Blackmon said.

Jack felt sick. This was going to be worse than anything in Vietnam. He wished the old man were there. Dexter would know what to do. Blackmon was going to have them killed as casually as he would shoot a snake.

"It ain't right," George said. "It's like killing a man for stealing watermelons."

"I bet you've done plenty of that," Blackmon said. "You don't get sent to prison for growing watermelons. They sell for considerably less than these plants."

"I got kin that'll come looking for me," George said.

"And they'll find nothing," Blackmon said. "No telling how far that river'll carry you before you're found. That's if the fishes and turtles don't get you first." Blackmon turned to Tudor. "Get them out of here."

"Wait," Jack said.

"Boy, this is not the time to go soft," Blackmon said.

"I'll do it," Jack said. "Haven't had the chance to waste anyone since 'Nam."

"We'll both go," Tudor said.

"Fuck off, little man," Jack said.

"No need to talk to him like that," Blackmon said.

Lonnie said, "We're just as good as you."

"Didn't say you weren't," Jack said. "Things like this are better done by one man. Something goes wrong and there's nobody but me to say what happened."

"Dexter would be proud of you," Blackmon said.

No, Jack thought. He would say I was being a fool. And this time he would be right.

Jack took out the .38 and gave George a shove in the direction of the sandbar.

"Give me any trouble and I'll drop you where you stand," Jack said.

"Take my flashlight," Blackmon said.

"No, thanks. I work better in the dark," Jack said.

Both men kept their mouths shut until they reached the sandbar.

"Please, mister," George said as they walked into the trees. "We won't tell."

"Keep moving," Jack said.

The stars were out, but there was no moon. George and Thomas were dark, featureless shapes, the sand squeaking under their feet. The river made a tearing sound as it slid past the sandbar. Upstream he heard the whine of the electric pump sucking water out of the river. They stopped at the edge of the water.

"We done nothing but steal a few plants," George said.

"Can't kill a man over that," Thomas said.

Jack wondered what Dexter would have done. He looked back at the dark mass of trees. Tudor was probably watching.

"I want you boys to forget the way to this place," Jack said. "You don't, that little man will find you and kill you."

"Jesus bless you," George said.

"Wouldn't be surprised if the little man was watching," Jack said. "I'm going to shoot past each of you. When I do, fall in the river. Swim for the Arkansas side."

"I can't swim so good," Thomas said. "Wait. I—"

Jack shot past Thomas first, but Thomas did not move. He shot again and George fell backward, taking Thomas with him. He fired two more rounds to make Blackmon and Tudor think he was making sure.

Instead of swimming as he had told them, they floated with the current along the curve of the sandbar. The darkness took them. He listened hard for sounds of swimming but heard nothing. Maybe it was going to be all right. Even Tudor would have little chance of finding them on the dark river.

He felt like crying. For a moment he had considered killing them. That was what Dexter would have done. Now he had put the whole community at risk. He wished that the river would rise and sweep the plants away, scour the field clean. He and Amy could go somewhere and buy land, maybe South America.

On the way back through the woods, he heard someone whistle ahead. Tudor stepped out from behind a tree and played the flashlight on him.

"You done a good job," Tudor said. "Smart making 'em walk down to the water. Nothing heavier than a dead man."

"Lots easier than greasing dinks," Jack said.

He followed Tudor through the trees to the cottonwood.

"You should've seen it," Tudor said.

"Stop," Blackmon said. "As far as I'm concerned, it never happened."

Tudor laughed.

"I didn't see nothing," Tudor said.

"Just remember, I wasn't here," Blackmon said.

Jack wondered if Tudor suspected.

"Where's Lonnie?" Jack asked.

"Watching the field," Tudor said. "Still plenty of thieves out there."

Jack and Blackmon started back for the lake. Frogs trilled from a puddle formed by runoff from the sprinklers.

"You can almost hear 'em growing," Blackmon said.

Jack did not answer and walking faster left Blackmon behind. He wanted to leave the smell of the plants behind just as sometimes he wanted to get away from Alligator's stink. The thought of executing the two men made him sick. If they had tried to run, he knew he probably would have shot them. Just as Alligator would attack another dog on sight. It felt good walking off into the darkness alone.

Blackmon caught up with him, breathing hard.

"I appreciate what you did," Blackmon said.

"It had to be done," Jack said.

Jack wondered if the men would go straight to the narcotics people. Or would they be too afraid of Tudor? They could have even drowned in the river. He found himself hoping they had. No one could be blamed for that.

From deep in the woods, Jack heard the shotgun. One, two shots. Then a pause and a third shot. But so far away they were no more than faint pops, the sound muffled by the trees. He knew what it was.

Jack watched Blackmon, who turned off the flashlight.

"That's Tudor doing what you couldn't," Blackmon said.

"They were too scared to talk," Jack said.

Jack felt as if he were being sucked under by one of those whirlpools that sometimes formed on the ends of the wing dams built to stabilize the river channel. It was dark and cold at the bottom of the river.

"Too much at stake to bet on that," Blackmon said.

"You bastard!" Jack shouted.

Jack wished Tudor were standing before him. He wanted to break the little man's bones.

Blackmon said, "Act like Dexter's son."

He took a step toward Blackmon, who swung the rifle on him.

"Think a minute," Blackmon said. "We all killed them."

"I didn't," Jack said.

"Law won't think so," Blackmon said. "Besides, they were trash. Nobody's going to care about them."

Jack tried to picture where the men lived. Probably in a trailer park.

"They were nothing," Blackmon said.

"Shut your goddamn mouth about them," Jack said.

Jack turned and ran toward the lake. He reached the boat and waited for Blackmon, mosquitoes buzzing about his ears. Blackmon took a long time coming out of the trees and when he did come it was slowly and without a light.

"You ready to go home?" Blackmon asked.

"No sense doing that. No sense doing any damn thing," Jack said.

"You be hard like Dexter," Blackmon said.

Jack said, "I'm not like him. Not like you."

"Let's go. Don't have time to listen to your whining."

Jack wanted to hit Blackmon but knew he was going to do nothing. It was too late. The men were dead. Trying to make it all come out different was like trying to turn Alligator into a lapdog.

As they crossed the lake, Jack running the motor and Blackmon sitting in the bow, Jack thought of the men being carried by the river. They might float all the way to the Gulf and come to rest on white sand in the clear green water, their bones picked clean by brightly colored fish.

Jack looked across the lake at the colored lights on Dumas's barge. He felt like turning the boat toward the lights, toward sweet Amy, and wrapping his arms about her he could find a place where he would be unable to hear the sound of the Hollandale boys' pleading voices.

Chapter Thirteen

Jack worked Alligator, the dog hotter in his hand than the sun on the back of his neck, and watched the collection tube slowly fill with semen.

"He loves you," Dexter said. "I wish I had me a woman loved me that much."

Squirrel laughed and said, "That dog loves nothing. Not even fighting. Just does it."

"Haven't you got enough?" Jack asked.

"Never have enough," Dexter said. "Squirrel says we may have to bring out another refrigerator."

Alligator still was indifferent to the whole process, even the electroejaculator. But the bitch took it seriously, squirming and howling in terror when they pulled Alligator's nose up to her.

They had gotten started late, and it was already hot, both dogs panting and the men covered with sweat. Dexter, who still wore his long-sleeved shirt buttoned at the collar, looked as if he had just stepped out of a shower. Now they had been three weeks without rain. Large cracks had formed in the ground, and the earth, baked dry by the fierce sun, had turned as hard as iron. Blackmon was running the pumps in the daytime.

They finished and Squirrel drew a blood sample from Alligator. Jack watched the needle fill with blood.

"For him it should be green or yellow. Like a bug," Jack said.

Evelyn came to the back door and told them breakfast would soon be ready. She was putting biscuits in the oven.

"Been getting some funny blood work on him," Squirrel said.

"Maybe I'll send a sample to the university lab at Jackson and have them run it on a gas chromatograph."

"What's that?" Dexter asked.

"Use it to detect traces of chemicals," Squirrel said.

"Something wrong?" Dexter asked. "Will he be able to fight?"

"He's fine. In great condition," Squirrel said. "I've just been wondering about it."

"Boy, what's Dumas been doing to that dog?" Dexter asked.

"Swimming him. Letting him swing on a rope," Jack said.

Jack was not going to tell Dexter about the rattlesnake venom. He did not believe that was what Squirrel was finding in Alligator's blood. But he liked knowing something about the training that Dexter did not.

"Nothing else?" Dexter asked.

"Nothing," Jack said. "Go talk to Dumas if you want."

Squirrel smelled Alligator, running his nose along his back.

"He smells different," Squirrel said.

Dexter sniffed at him too.

"Smells like he always does," Dexter said. "Stinks."

"It's what the bitch is afraid of," Squirrel said.

"She's afraid of getting killed," Dexter said.

Jack heard a car come into the driveway. A white Mercedes appeared around the corner of the house. Billy Ray was at the wheel, and Mike Jaban sat beside him.

"Friends of yours?" Dexter asked.

"I know them," Jack said.

"Business then," Dexter said.

"My business," Jack said.

Jack thought about going to the house for a gun. But it was too late. They got out of the car. Jaban looked as if he had just come off the golf course, his blue-black hair shining in the sun. Billy Ray wore a green jumpsuit.

"I've come for her," Jaban said.

Jack said, "She's not here."

"You find her," Jaban said.

"Hold on," Dexter said.

Billy Ray took a step toward Dexter. Jaban put his hand on Billy Ray's arm and stopped him.

"Let him come on," Dexter said. And then he turned to Jack. "You owe this man a gambling debt?"

"No, sir," Jack said.

"You cut or shoot some of his kin?"

"No, sir."

"You tomcatting with his wife?"

"No, sir."

Dexter walked up close to Jaban and said, "Get off my place."

"I'm asking you one more time," Jaban said to Jack. "Where's Amy?"

"Amy!" Dexter said. "Amy the nurse?"

Dexter began to laugh.

"Boy, you are dumb beyond belief," Dexter said. Then to Jaban, "I told you to leave."

"Breakfast," Evelyn called from the back door.

Nobody even looked at her. She went inside.

"He knows where she is," Jaban said, pointing at Jack. "She belongs to me."

Evelyn came out into the yard. She wore an apron.

"The eggs will be getting cold," she said to Dexter. "Are these gentlemen staying for breakfast?"

"They're leaving," Dexter said. "Right now."

"I'm asking you one last time," Jaban said to Jack. "Where's Amy?"

Billy Ray stepped forward and put his hand on Dexter's arm. Jaban retreated to the car.

"Tell me or I'll break his arm," Billy Ray said to Jack.

"Go ahead," Jack said. "I've tried plenty of times myself."

"Jack," Evelyn said.

Jack decided he was going to do nothing. Dexter would find out he had gotten too old for brawling.

Squirrel left Alligator and ran forward with the dog's chain in his hand. He reached Dexter and Billy Ray just as the old man, moving quicker than Jack thought he could, brought his knee up into Billy Ray's groin. Billy Ray sighed, and as he started to fall, Squirrel caught him across the nose with the chain. Blood spurted, and Billy Ray went down hard.

Jack looked toward the car and saw Jaban bringing the sawed-off shotgun up on them. Evelyn pulled her pistol out from beneath her apron and put one round through the back window. Jaban disappeared behind the seat.

"The next one goes between your eyes!" Evelyn shouted. "Throw out that gun!"

Jaban hesitated, then opened the door and threw the gun out on the ground.

Billy Ray slowly sat up, the blood streaming down his face. Jack saw Alligator run past and thought he was going for Billy Ray. But instead he went for the car and took a hold on a front tire. Alligator shook the tire, making the whole car sway, the shocks creaking and the dog breathing hard as he worked his teeth deeper into the tire. A trickle of foam appeared at one side of his mouth and darkened the rubber.

"Stop him!" Jaban shouted.

The air went out of the tire with a hiss, and Alligator released his hold, stepping back from the tire as if it were a snake. As soon as the hissing stopped, he went to the next one and began to shake it. The dog methodically destroyed each tire. Billy Ray sat very still on the ground and watched.

"Don't turn that dog on me," Billy Ray said over and over.

"Be still," Dexter said.

When Alligator had destroyed the last tire, he trotted over and lay down in the shade of a pecan tree. Squirrel put the chain back on him.

Billy Ray got up and, keeping an eye on Alligator, took a seat behind the wheel.

Jaban said, "How're we going to get home?"

"You're going to drive," Dexter said.

"Tires are flat," Jaban said.

"Drive," Dexter said.

"Tell her she better come back," Jaban said to Jack.

"She'll do what she wants," Jack said.

Dexter said, "I'm not asking you to leave again."

Billy Ray drove the car out of the yard, running on the rims. They could tell when it reached the road by the clank of metal on the asphalt.

"Where is she?" Dexter asked.

"You planning on striking up her acquaintance again?" Jack asked.

Dexter said nothing. Squirrel went off to prepare the semen for the refrigerator. Alligator was back on the wire and had crawled up in the shade of his shelter. Jack wondered why they were all standing out in the open, letting the sun bake their brains out.

"Why are you so interested in every woman I've known?" Dexter asked. "You want to hump every one of them? You're young. Good-looking. Could have most any girl you want."

Evelyn walked toward the house.

"Wait," Dexter said. "I didn't mean—"

"The eggs are getting cold," she said.

"We'll be in right away," Dexter said.

Squirrel followed Evelyn into the house.

"Where is she?" Dexter asked.

"With Dumas," Jack said.

"Goddamn, are you crazy? That little hooker is just out for money. Probably stole something from that Lebanese. He didn't come all the way out here to get himself killed over love."

"I love her."

"You broke the first rule. Fuck 'em but don't fall in love. Alligator's got more sense than you."

"Yeah, he tries to kill 'em. You're the one who sent me up there to her."

"That was because you sneaked out and spied on me and Evelyn."

"Do you love Evelyn?"

"I like her. She likes me," Dexter said. He looked up at the sun as if he were planning to stare at it until he went blind. "I loved your mother."

Jack laughed, making Alligator pick his head up and rattle his chain.

"You can't love," Jack said. "No more than that dog can."

"I built this place to leave something to you."

"And you lost it. You didn't build it for me. All it ever meant to you was money for your women."

"Come and eat," Evelyn called from the back door.

Dexter sent her back inside with a wave of his hand.

"She's the right kind of woman for you," Jack said. "Meaner than any man I've ever met except you."

Dexter said, "That's enough."

"Do you and her talk about Mother in bed?" Jack said. "Laugh about how you ran her off?"

Dexter lunged toward him, but Jack easily stepped aside. The old man moved like a crippled bear. His fight with Billy Ray had finished him.

"You're too old to take me," Jack said. "I'll own this land in a few months."

"All of you are going to end up in jail," Dexter said as he circled Jack.

"Forget it, old man," Jack said. "I'm not that little Lebanese. You can't touch me."

Dexter made a move for him, tripped, and fell. He lay gasping for breath.

"How's it feel to be old?" Jack said.

Dexter slowly pushed himself up on one knee and then stood, swaying before him, the sweat dripping off his face.

"Stop it! Stop it!" Evelyn screamed, running toward them.

Alligator watched them with his ears raised.

"That's your real son," Jack said, pointing to the dog. "And you won't be satisfied until he's dead. Well, he won't die. He's going to beat that Firecracker dog."

"I hope so," Dexter said.

"No, you want him dead. Everything dead."

Jack walked off and took Alligator off the cable. He sniffed at the dog as he did it, trying to smell what Squirrel had. But the dog smelled the same to him. Evelyn took Dexter inside, and Jack put Alligator in the truck. He headed for the lake and Amy.

Chapter Fourteen

J ack put Alligator over the side of the boat to cool off, the dog swimming through patches of green duckweed. Jack took off his shirt and splashed water on his chest, tracing the shrapnel scars with his fingers. When he pulled Alligator back into the boat, the dog put his cold wet nose up against his chest and sniffed at the scars.

"Smell that old blood?" Jack said. "Or can you read 'em? Amy said you could."

Alligator shook, spraying him. Bits of duckweed remained stuck to the dog's coat.

"Don't need to know," he said. "Already know all there is about dying."

Jack hugged the shoreline to take advantage of small patches of shade. They reached the slough, which was a dark tunnel, protected from the sun by interlaced tree branches. At their approach, turtles and snakes slid off logs where they had been basking in patches of sunlight. A blue heron took wing from a patch of grass and flapped slowly out of sight around a bend in the slough.

From Carrie he learned Dumas and Amy had gone snake hunting.

"Never seen someone take to snakes like her," Carrie said.

"Knows kin when she sees them," Jack said.

"Don't you treat that little girl mean."

"She can take care of herself."

"You fighting?"

"Not yet."

Carrie chuckled and said, "People in love always fight."

"I'm not in love with her. I'd just as soon sleep in a bed full of rattlesnakes."

"You're in love all right," Carrie said. "Got all the signs."

"Watch out for her."

"Why'd you bring her out here?"

"She's got trouble."

"You've made her trouble yours. That's love."

Jack wondered if Carrie was right, if it was too late to rid himself of Amy. She had warned him over and over, made no secret of what she was. But what made him the maddest was the good laugh Dexter was getting out of the whole affair.

"Which way did they go?" Jack asked.

"Up towards where that tornado came through last year," Carrie said.

Jack ran the boat up the slough until he came to the place where the tornado had crossed it. It was as if a road had been hastily cut through the woods by one of those big jungle-clearing machines he had seen in Vietnam, the big trees snapped off, sometimes at the base and sometimes halfway up, the piles of logs forming an impassable tangle. He saw Dumas's boat pulled up on the bank.

He landed and walked into the trees, allowing the dog to run free. The dry leaves crackled under his feet, Alligator making casts out in front of him. Jack picked his way through the briars and vines, the ground hard under his feet, and everywhere he caught that low-water smell of wet leaves and logs and of the earth slowly drying in the sun. Mosquitoes hummed in his ears as he crossed a dry creekbed. Alligator scrambled up the far bank. He called to the dog, afraid Alligator was going to get overheated.

As he came up out of the creekbed, he heard voices. Alligator stood motionless, watching Dumas and Amy.

"Hey, dog," Dumas yelled.

Alligator ran for Dumas. Amy stepped behind the old man, her earrings flashing. They stood in a clearing where broom sedge and clumps of blackberries grew. Amy held a plastic milk jug half full of gas. Dumas had a snake bag on his belt and carried an aluminum snake pole that had a wire loop set in the end. One of the Memphis doctors he guided for deer in the winter and took on snake hunts in the summer had given it to him.

"Tie him up," Amy said.

Dumas started to take the dog by the collar.

Jack said, "Let him be."

Alligator sniffed Amy's leg.

"Get away!" Amy said.

Alligator went rigid and looked up at her as if he were trying to make up his mind whether to take a bite out of one of those long, tanned legs that were now covered with mosquito bites.

"He stinks," Amy said. "Jack, get him away."

Alligator trotted off into the trees.

"That dog gets lost, your daddy'll skin us both," Dumas said.

"He won't go far," Jack said. "Likes Amy too much."

"I'll get him," Dumas said, walking off through the trees and calling to Alligator.

"Jaban came looking for you," Jack said.

"I don't care what he does," Amy said.

"Billy Ray was with him. You sure cared when you showed up the other day."

"They won't come out here."

"What'd you do? Steal the family silver?"

"I don't steal."

"You tell him you'd fuck him and nobody else?"

Amy pouted and played with an earring.

"All you care about is that dog," she said.

Alligator walked out of the trees and flopped down in the shade, to pant with his tongue hanging out. Dumas called for him from the woods, and Alligator raised his ears.

"Keep him away," Amy said.

"He's too hot to bother you," Jack said.

Jack heard Dumas coming through the trees.

"You must have done something," Jack said.

"Mike wants me all for himself," Amy said. "Just like you. I don't want that. I told him. I told you. Won't either of you believe me."

Her face was covered with sweat. She looked as if she were going to start crying.

"Stay away from Jaban," Jack said.

"Don't tell me what to do," she said.

"You planning on taking on Billy Ray?"

"I can take care of myself."

Alligator yawned and rolled about, rubbing his back against the ground.

"That dog wants to bite me," she said.

"No, he wants to fight other dogs. He's not much interested in people."

Dumas came out of the trees and saw Alligator.

"Dog don't pay me no mind," he said. "After all the time I spent with him." Dumas picked up the jug of gasoline. "Let's catch us a snake."

Dumas led them to a hole in the center of the clearing. The broom sedge was beaten down where something had been going in and out. Alligator sniffed at the hole and then trotted over and lay down under a big oak. Jack remembered tunnels in Vietnam, but he never had to go down into them. They always picked some little skinny guy.

"Scaly pig made that hole," Dumas said. "Then a big serpent moved in. Snake won't bother breaking his tusks on scales."

"What's a scaly pig?" Amy asked.

"Armadillo," Jack said.

Dumas took the jug and poured some of the gasoline down the hole.

"We'll see who's at home," Dumas said. "Fumes'll give mister snake a big headache."

They all crouched close to the hole. The gas had stained the earth dark around the entrance. Dumas held the aluminum pole. Amy fixed her eyes on the hole. She had not bothered to wipe the sweat off her face. The emerald earrings caught the sunlight, flashing green.

"She got a way with serpents," Dumas said. "Just like you got with dogs."

Jack heard a faint scratching sound from deep in the hole.

"Move back," Dumas said. "He knows we're here. Can feel us moving."

Jack stepped back with Amy, wanting to move into the shade with Alligator, but Amy took his arm, her fingers circling his wrist.

"Wait," she said.

"It's too hot," he said.

He pulled away and walked to the shade. She remained in the sun, watching Dumas, who stood perhaps ten feet away from the hole. Jack had seen Dumas catch plenty of snakes.

She moved closer, but Dumas raised his hand and stopped her. Alligator had gone to sleep. Jack preferred the stink of the dog to that of the gasoline.

The snake's head appeared, a big rattler, diamond patterned yellow and brown, flowing out of the darkness into the light. It shook its bell. Amy held her hands to her face in an attitude of prayer. Dumas waited until the snake had cleared the hole, all six feet of it sliding smoothly across the bare ground toward a clump of blackberry bushes, and slipped the loop over its head.

Immediately the snake began to fight with its rattles buzzing, its mouth open wide, hissing and throwing coils about the pole, which bent under its weight.

"Get his head," Dumas said to Amy.

But as she stepped forward, Dumas tripped and went down hard. The snake slipped out of the loop and coiled, its rattles making a fierce buzz, its head only a foot or so from the old man's. Jack took a step and stopped, afraid any movement would provoke the snake into striking. He heard the cicadas in the trees and felt the sun on his face and smelled the dry grass. Amy had closed her eyes. It was as if Dumas were never going to move and the snake were never going to uncoil and Amy were never going to open her eyes, all three like a grouping created by some mad sculptor. Dumas rolled away and got slowly to his feet, the snake remaining coiled. Amy picked up the pole.

"Let me," she said.

"No," Dumas said. "He had his chance at me. Now I'm gonna put him in the sack."

Dumas slipped the loop over the snake's head again, stooping low to the ground and bracing himself against the struggle he knew was coming. The snake twisted and hissed, but this time Dumas held on. Gradually the snake tired and was still.

"Take him," Dumas said to Amy.

She took his head, and Dumas released the wire loop. While Dumas held the sack open, she started to drop the snake into it. Jack walked over to stand beside them.

"Want to hold him?" Amy asked Jack.

"Not me," Jack said.

"You afraid?"

"I don't like snakes."

"They're beautiful."

Dumas said, "Put him in the sack, honey."

Jack could smell the snake, a musty odor, mixed with the scent of Amy's sweat. Her earrings flashed in the sunlight.

"You like that dog because he kills things," Amy said. "Dumas says snakes just kill to eat. This snake wouldn't kill anything for you. You couldn't train him."

The snake buzzed and coiled its tail around Amy's arm.

"In the sack," Dumas said.

"That dog's scared of him too," Amy said. "Just like you."

She walked toward Alligator with the snake.

"Here, dog," she said.

Alligator stood up, Jack started after her.

"Don't fool with that dog," he said.

Jack saw Alligator's eyes glaze over. The dog took a step toward Amy and she, holding the snake's twisting body high over her head with both arms extended, threw it at Alligator.

"Fight that!" she screamed.

Before the snake had a chance to coil, Alligator was on it, moving faster than Jack believed was possible, and took it by the head, shaking it and the head crunching beneath his teeth. The dog finally released it, the snake's body still twitching.

"You bitch," Jack said. "If he's been bit . . ."

"Won't matter," Dumas said. "He's poison proofed."

"I hope he dies," Amy said.

Alligator turned to her at the sound of her voice. Jack knew he was going for her and moved before the dog did, leaving his feet just as Alligator started. He tackled the dog as he once had brought down halfbacks on a football field, except that instead of the smell of pads and sweat and grass there was the stink of Alligator.

He grabbed his collar, but Jack was afraid he was not going to be able to hold him. The dog's determination to get at Amy made him more afraid than anything he had experienced in Vietnam. He had never been afraid of Alligator before, just careful. Maybe she was right about the dog. He should be destroyed before he killed someone. Alligator was twisting away from him when Jack picked him up off the ground, the dog's back to him. Alligator's legs flailed at the air. He could feel the dog's heat, the sag of his guts beneath the muscle. He held his jaws closed with one hand.

"Kill him, kill him!" Amy screamed.

Dumas came and pulled Amy away.

"Take her home," Jack said.

It was all Amy's fault. He might end up losing an arm to Alligator, and it was the girl who had stirred him up.

Dumas led Amy away. Jack was left holding Alligator in an embrace, waiting for the dog to calm down, the dog's breathing getting slower and slower as the craziness went out of him, Jack holding him tighter than any lover in the dry grass beneath the fierce sun.

Chapter Fifteen

Tudor and his kin culled the male plants, leaving the females to put out flower after flower, raising huge colas, as the plants readied themselves for the pollen that was not going to appear. And on the land no longer his, Jack watched them preparing to harvest beans and cotton. Robert Red flew early each morning, spraying defoliant on the cotton. Jack had started running Alligator on one of the treadmills. By October he would begin to taper off the workouts as the time for the fight drew closer.

In the early-morning cool, wisps of fog still hanging low over the grass, Jack worked Alligator on the catmill, the dog chasing the fanged monster's face in circles. Jack wondered if the dog knew he was chasing a rubber mask or if he simply wanted to do battle with something that looked meaner than any dog he had ever fought.

Blackmon's truck came into the yard.

"We got trouble," Blackmon said.

"Tudor smoke up all the crop?" Jack asked.

Blackmon jabbed a finger toward the south and said, "There's a hurricane out in the Gulf. Comes up this way the field'll flood."

The kitchen timer Jack had set for the catmill went off. Alligator stopped.

"You and Dumas are going to set too fine of an edge on that dog," Blackmon said, shaking his head. "The Firecracker trains by killing other men's dogs."

"Long about Halloween we'll see," Jack said.

"We need sandbags," Blackmon said. "Have to go to Memphis for them."

"Maybe it won't come up this way."

"It does and it rains enough and the wind blows hard, we could lose everything."

"Go to Memphis then."

"I will. We'll have to all go out there and wait for the storm if it heads this way. Lake'll be too rough to cross once it hits. Maybe I'll take a front-end loader out there."

Blackmon left for Memphis. Jack went into the house and turned on the TV. The morning news was on, and the weather girl pointed out the swirl of clouds out in the Gulf that was the hurricane. Headed for New Orleans.

Jack thought of Amy. He would have to get her off the lake. But Dumas had ridden out bad storms before. He would know what to do. She would be safe.

Dexter came into the room.

"Risked going to Parchman and now the storm could take it all," Dexter said.

"You'd like that," Jack said.

"No. Blackmon gone for sandbags?"

"Won't do any good."

"Will if you put 'em along the creek. That's where the water always comes from. Won't affect the river much. Go down about as fast as it comes up. That way you'll only lose the north end. Nothing can save that."

"Come and help."

"No, thanks. Don't want to spend the next ten years growing cotton for the state."

Jack wished Dexter were with them. Blackmon was scared. But maybe Dexter would have been scared too if the crop were his. He could stay calm because he cared about nothing. That was his edge.

They watched the hurricane on TV for the next few days. It

made a move toward Mobile and then changed course for New Orleans again and strengthened. Finally it came ashore and blew itself out in the marshes west of New Orleans, the remnants tracking northeast through Louisiana.

Blackmon stockpiled sandbags on the island. When the clouds began to build up, they went out to the field to wait for the storm.

Tudor had brought a couple of johnboats up from the lake in case the whole island went underwater. He sat in one watching the clouds and smoking a huge joint, the tip glowing red, the smoke trailing away in a bluish plume. Blackmon had used a front-end loader to bring sand up from the river. A hill of it was on the south end of the field. With the front-end loader, he had raised a low levee along the creek. They would use the sandbags to repair leaks or breaks.

Robert Red took a long drink from a pint bottle of Wild Turkey.

"Fucking Noah's ark is what we need," Robert Red said.

Blackmon looked up from a portable weather radio.

"They say it won't be that bad," Blackmon said, looking up at the sky.

Robert Red threw his hands up in the air and said, "We'll get washed down the river. End up in New Orleans. Can't even speak Cajun."

"You said the water'd never get that high," Norris complained to Blackmon.

Norris retied the laces on a pair of knee-high rubber boots.

"Leave if you want," Blackmon said to Norris. "It'll come off your share."

"And Sally Ann would kick his ass," Wade said.

They all laughed.

Jack saw Dumas and Amy come up the track by the edge of the field.

"Who's he bringing out here?" Blackmon asked.

"I know her," Jack said.

"We came to help," Dumas said. "Carrie's staying with her sister in Greenville."

Amy was dressed in jeans, a work shirt, and a pair of new rubber hip boots. She looked good.

"We're not giving you a share," Blackmon said to Amy.

"Leave her alone," Jack said.

Blackmon said, "She wants a share. Let it come out of yours."

They went to the pile of sand and started filling sandbags. Blackmon carried the bags along the edge of the field with the front-end loader.

Amy held bags open while Jack filled them.

"I'm sorry about the dog," Amy said.

"Snake missed," Jack said.

"Dumas says snakes can't hurt him," she said.

"Crazy old man," Jack said. "He can feed Alligator all the rattlesnake venom he wants. Won't make any difference. Alligator's going to fight dogs, not snakes."

"I told you I'd do something like that," she said. "I told you."

"Be quiet."

"You've been sweet to me. Said nice things. But I told you."

Jack thought of her in bed and got a hard-on as he dug the shovel into the sand. He knew he was not going to be able to stay away from her, no matter how many times she warned him. But maybe she was saying one thing and wanting another.

"How many times are you-all going to fill that sandbag?" Robert Red asked, smoking a joint now that his whiskey was gone. "Wind'll probably blow my hangar down tonight. Do I care? Hell, no. Blackmon says we're all going to be rich. Underwater is what we're going to be."

They filled sandbags until dark. Other men from the community had appeared. Travis was there, complaining Blackmon had not built the levee right. The principal had brought most of his black neighbors with him.

"You got to slope it more," Travis said to Blackmon.

"It'll hold," Blackmon said.

When it grew dark, they lit lanterns and continued to work. No rain had fallen yet but the wind had grown stronger. They stopped work to eat under a tarp Tudor rigged up beneath one of the big cottonwoods. They ate food Francis had brought from his store: cheese, sausage, crackers, and sardines. Blackmon turned up the weather radio, and they listened to the flash-flood warnings being issued for counties to the south.

Someone wearing a carbide headlamp came along the track. It was Evelyn. She had almost swamped coming across the lake. She and Amy hugged each other like a couple of sorority sisters at a homecoming reunion. Jack still could not understand why Evelyn did not hate Amy.

A tornado warning came over the weather radio.

"Tornados," Norris said. "I forgot about tornados."

Norris sat down and held his hands over his head.

"Be a man," Blackmon said.

"My daddy went through the Greenwood tornado," Norris said. "Said there were dead niggers hanging in the trees after it was over. Don't want to end up dead in a tree."

"Can't go back," Evelyn said. "You'd drown for sure."

It began to rain. Off in the distance a flash of lightning lit up the sky as they waited under the tarp for the creek to rise. Tudor prowled the creekbank, returning now and then to report to Blackmon. He still held the huge joint between his teeth, but it had been put out by the wind-driven rain.

"It's coming up," Tudor said.

The whites of his little black eyes were so red and swollen that they seemed to glow in the lantern light. It was near midnight. Nobody slept.

Blackmon organized them into squads, and they spread out along the creekbank. He put Jack, Evelyn, and Amy together.

"You're going to do all this work for nothing," Blackmon said to Amy.

"You won't owe me," Amy said.

The lower north end of the field was already partially underwater, but the south half was on higher ground and could be saved if they could keep the creek out of it. In the light from flashlights and lanterns, Jack saw some of the plants had been uprooted by the strong gusts while the tops of others had been broken off. He turned his back to the driving rain and felt it beat against his waterproof duck-hunting coat. The water in the creek slid by, the surface littered with leaves and sticks and limbs torn loose by the wind.

Evelyn stood beside him at the base of the levee while Amy played her flashlight on the swollen creek.

"Dexter's probably asleep in a warm bed somewhere," Jack said.

"Why can't you leave it alone?" said Evelyn.

"Don't understand why you don't care," he said.

"You took up with Amy," she said. "Don't you care?"

"That's different."

She laughed and said, "I hear a man talking."

Evelyn glanced up at Amy to see if she was trying to listen, but Amy had her eyes fixed on the rising brown water.

"He's still in love with Margaret," Evelyn said.

"What about you?" Jack asked.

"We like each other. He loved Margaret. Won't ever love anybody else."

Jack tried to think of a reason why Evelyn would lie.

"I've always been jealous of Margaret," Evelyn went on. "Used to hate her for Dexter's love."

"Now you're getting even," Jack said.

"No, there's nothing I can do. He's always going to love her," Evelyn said.

Jack could not imagine Dexter loving anyone unless it was one of his dogs.

"Look, a drowned deer," Amy said from the top of the levee. "Poor thing."

"It's the truth," Evelyn said.

She climbed the levee to stand with Amy.

Jack first understood about Dexter's women when he turned twelve and was allowed to go bird hunting. He remembered the weight of the shells in his vest, the tug of briars against his legs, the red leaves of the sumacs, the limp birds he took out of the dogs' mouths; it all seemed like a dream, played before his eyes on warm November afternoons in the soft autumn light. He loved the old man then. He kept track of the birds he shot by marking down the day's bag on the calendar in the kitchen.

Then early one morning before a hunt Dexter stopped off in Greenville. The old man told him to wait in the truck with the dogs, who whined impatiently from the dogbox. He petted the dogs through the wire and walked up and down the sidewalk to keep warm because he had dressed light for fast walking.

He went up on the porch and sat in the sun, watching the frost disappear from the lawn. Then he went to the door and opened the screen. He gave the door a push. It swung open, and he paused, listening for the deep, rich sound of Dexter's voice. The house was silent. As he stepped inside, the room warm from a gas heater, he heard the sound, rhythmical and heavy. He went down the hall, following the sound, until through the partially open bedroom door he saw his father's broad back and the pair of legs wrapped around his waist.

Back out on the porch he sat looking at trees and grass and sky as if for the first time. He wanted to cry but did not because the old man would mock him if he found him crying. The dogs whined from the truck. He squinted his eyes against the sun that now rose over the trees and wished he had not seen the two entwined together.

"Thought I told you to stay in the truck," Dexter said.

He looked up at him dressed in his hunting clothes, huge as always, so big that Jack always wondered if it was going to be possible for him to grow that tall. But already he was a head above any boy in his class at school.

"I got cold," he said.

"Next time do as you're told," Dexter said.

They drove out of town, Jack grateful the old man made no excuses like how he was collecting a gambling debt or seeing a friend. He said nothing. Dexter had the scent of the woman on him, a smell of lilacs.

When the dogs pointed the first covey, one with his nose down in the grass and the other backing, the old man motioned him in to kick up the birds. Jack would get the best shots, and the old man would kill whatever he missed.

"Pick out single birds," Dexter said. "Don't shoot blind into the covey."

He had seen Dexter kill five birds on a covey rise with the Browning, shooting the first one just as the birds got off the ground, killing every bird cleanly. It always seemed like magic to him. He did not think he would ever be able to shoot that well. Sometimes he made doubles, but he had to concentrate hard to do it.

As he walked slowly past the trembling dog, the birds went up with a whir. He never raised his gun, the new 20-gauge he had received for his birthday. When the covey swung to his right, his father dropped two birds.

"We came out here to shoot birds," the old man said.

The dogs searched for the downed birds. He turned and faced Dexter. And for the first time he experienced the desire to kill his father, the metal taste of fear and rage in his mouth, his fingers tightening around the shotgun. It would be so easy. A hunting accident. That's what he could say had happened.

"You put it on yourself," the old man said, unafraid as always. "Next time you'll do as I say."

He turned and went off to follow the dogs as they hunted up the singles. During the rest of the day he shot better than he ever had before, not missing a bird and making three doubles.

"Up here," someone yelled.

They ran for the break, the brown water bubbling up at the base of the levee. They began piling sandbags on the break. Up and down the length of the levee, other breaks began to appear.

"You didn't pack the dirt down right," Travis said to Blackmon.

"I'm not the goddamn Corps of Engineers," Blackmon said. They started to run out of sandbags. Amy, Evelyn, and Dumas filled them while the younger men carried them to the weak points. The creek was now high over its banks, spreading out into the trees. They kept stacking sandbags on the levee. Soon they had covered almost the entire outer face of the levee with sandbags and were beginning to lay bags on the top. Blackmon tried to use the front-end loader, but it became hopelessly mired in the mud, which also sucked at Jack's boots when he tried to walk. Jack found he was soaked with sweat and took off his rain gear. As long as he kept moving, he was able to keep warm. Tudor had taken off his boots and was working barefoot. Travis was dressed in a yellow raincoat that had "School Safety Patrol" written in fluorescent letters across the back. Every time the wind rose, Norris started worrying about tornados.

Amy had fallen, her face streaked with mud and her long blond hair dark with mud and water. Evelyn's hip boots were muddy, but she had managed to stay clean and dry in a blue rainsuit. The water continued to rise, and they frantically piled bags on the levee, staggering under their loads and slipping in the mud. The rain continued, and the creek rose quickly to near the top of the levee.

Occasionally a chunk of the levee would drop off into the water, making a sucking sound, the ground trembling beneath their feet. They dropped sandbags in to fill the hole, the bags hitting the dark water with heavy splashes, causing eddies and swirls in the current. Jack was so tired he could hardly walk. Amy and Evelyn were still filling sandbags. Dumas had given out and was asleep under the tarp.

In the early hours of the morning, as the rain fell harder and the wind tore at the trees, making it sound as if a tornado were bearing down upon them, Jack put his hand on the levee and felt it vibrating.

"Stop, touch it!" Jack shouted.

They all put their hands on the levee. The vibration increased so, Jack could feel it through his boots.

"It's going to break!" Norris shouted.

"More sandbags," Blackmon yelled.

Jack felt the levee move under his feet. Then suddenly earth changed to water, and he and Norris were swept backwards into the fence. For a moment Jack was pinned against the wire, his head pulled underwater. He dragged himself up on the wire, searching in the darkness for the surface. He broke through, gasping for air, sticks and branches pushed against his chest by the current. A cluster of lights marked the break.

"Jack! Jack!" Norris shouted.

The sound came from above him in the darkness. He worked his way along the fence until he was out of the water.

Norris continued to call for help until finally someone on the levee heard him over the rush of the water. They shined a light through the trees. Jack saw Norris perched in the fork of a tree only a few feet above the water, a small wave topped with foam surging against the tree trunk.

"Swim for it," Jack yelled.

Norris shook his head and tightened his grip on the tree.

Blackmon appeared with a rope, which he had to throw three times before Norris could be persuaded to let go of the tree and catch it. Norris made the rope fast to the tree, and they anchored it to another tree.

"Monkey-crawl," Blackmon shouted.

Norris put a hand on the rope but hesitated.

"Crawl or I'll cut it," Blackmon yelled, taking out a knife. "You can rot up there."

Norris made no move for the rope. The wind gusted in the trees. Lightning flashed.

"Tornado's coming," Jack shouted.

Norris came across the rope, his legs wrapped around it and his arms pumping. He slipped, falling face-down in the mud. The wind died. Norris looked up at them, Blackmon playing the flashlight on his face.

"You tricked me," Norris complained. "I could've drowned."

"You dumb shit," Blackmon said.

"I could have drowned," Norris kept saying as he stumbled through the darkness behind them.

They returned to the break, where the others were dropping sandbags into the breach. Jack carried sandbags until his arms and legs felt numb and his whole body ached. Finally they succeeded in wedging logs in the opening and sealing the break by dropping sandbags among them.

Morning came, the brown water only a foot below the top row of sandbags. Everyone was covered with mud and had the same vacant stares on their faces Jack had seen in combat. He traced his scars through his wet T-shirt. The heavy rain continued until midafternoon, when it changed to a steady drizzle. They were out of sandbags. Blackmon's weather radio had gone out during the night so they had no idea if more rain was on the way.

"Must have just caught the edge of it," Blackmon said. "We saved half the field. Still make plenty off it."

Amy and Evelyn sat on the sand, which had been reduced to a low mound instead of a hill. Travis emptied water out of his boots, standing first on one foot and then on the other. Norris, still worried about tornados, was trying to repair the weather radio. Blackmon and Wade walked up and down the length of the levee, inspecting it for leaks. Tudor had rolled a new joint and was passing it around among his kin, who looked as if they had all been stamped out with the same die: stoop-shouldered, lean-assed men.

They all walked into the field, the mud up to their knees and sucking at their boots. The north end of the field was underwater, most of the plants beaten down and washed away. Jack watched a water snake swim away through the ruined plants, its head lifted and its body moving in smooth loops. The break had sent a stream of water into the field that had scoured out a channel through the earth, ripping plants out of the ground. But most of the plants were still standing.

Tudor set a plant upright, its huge cola covered with mud. It stayed a moment, but a gust of wind toppled it.

"No bone in it," Tudor said as he cut off the cola. "Dry this and it'll be fine."

But when he picked it up, the soaked cola fell apart in his hands.

"Soft as baby shit," Tudor said.

He began to gather up the buds, picking them out of the mud and placing them in his open palm.

Jack felt pride in what they had done. He had thought they would lose the whole field. There were still plenty of plants left. By this time next year he could be working his own land, watching beans and cotton push up out of the rich black soil.

Chapter Sixteen

Amy and Jack drifted in the johnboat along the slough at dusk. Alligator sat at Jack's feet. She had been swimming and was combing out her hair. Somewhere honeysuckle was blooming, and the sweet smell mixed with the stink of the dog and the water scent of Amy's wet hair. During her swim, the dog had watched her as if she were an opponent being brought into the pit.

"I'm going to New Orleans," she said.

"Jaban'll find you."

"It's not like he's the Mafia," she said. "I'm not scared of him."

"He's out there," Jack said. "Waiting."

"Nothing here for me," she said.

"I am."

"Why, you're broke. Dumas is better off than you."

"This time next year I'll own my own land."

"I've got friends in New Orleans."

He wondered why he wanted her to stay. She had warned him not to trust her, not to love her. And maybe he did not care for her at all. Maybe she was just a way of getting even with the old man. Dexter had known how to handle her. Pay her off and get out.

"You can have part of my share," he said, knowing he was a fool for offering her anything.

"How much?"

"A share of the farm."

She shook her head. "What do I want with a bunch of dirt? How much?"

"More than Dexter ever gave you," he said.

"I'll stay for a while," she said. "Make that dog stop looking at me."

Jack petted Alligator on the top of his head.

"You tried to hurt him," Jack said. "He won't forget."

Back at the barge Amy decided she wanted to go to the Duck Club. It was a private nightclub, all glass and redwood, built beside the lake. Blackmon was a member. So was Dexter, but he hardly ever went there.

They left Alligator chained on the barge and took the boat up the lake.

"I want me a mixed drink," Amy said. "I want to dance. I wish I had a nice dress."

He steered for the cluster of lights that was the Duck Club. Amy sat in the stern with her long hair blowing in the wind, looking white against the blackness.

They found Robert Red tending bar and watching the Braves play on TV. When the crop-dusting season was over, he managed the club. Amy ordered a tequila sunrise and Jack a beer. Her emerald earrings glittered in the bar lights as she drank it.

"This is nice," Amy said.

"We got tennis courts and a place to have barbecue out by the water," Robert Red said. "Membership is down. Nobody's got any money. If it wasn't for the slot machines, we'd go broke."

"Once the crop's made, you won't be able to get a seat in here," Jack said.

"I'm going to buy me a club on the coast," Robert Red said. "You think Biloxi or Gulfport would be better?"

"Just make sure it's in Harrison County," Amy said. "Sheriff'll let you do anything down there. You can have gambling, girls. Make sure you're close to the beach."

Jack drained half the beer in one long swallow. Amy sipped at her drink. They watched Horner strike out with two men on base.

"They always lose," Robert Red said.

"They need better pitching," Jack said.

"I didn't come here to watch a baseball game," Amy said. "Where's the band?"

"No band tonight," Robert Red said. "Only on Saturday."

"Let's go someplace else," she said.

"Take us the rest of the night to get to Greenville by boat," Jack said.

Amy pouted. When she finished her drink, Jack took her across the empty dance floor. In a corner behind the bandstand was all that remained of his old high school. He turned on a light and showed her the football trophies and pictures of the team. She picked him out in the pictures. There were two large pictures of players who had gone off to have good careers at Ole Miss.

"Why didn't you play in college?" she asked.

"Had two running backs who were faster than me," he said.

"Scared you wouldn't get to play?"

"I guess so."

"I'm glad you didn't play. Baby, you're too pretty to get your face all busted up."

She stroked his cheek.

"Dammit, I told you not to call me that."

"Don't care if you played," she said. "Don't even like football."

"We'll go to the Founders Club," he said. "I'm always lucky on the slot machine there."

They got the key from Robert Red and opened a metal gate at the head of a flight of stairs. They went down to a small room with a polished wooden table in the center, a small dance floor, a jukebox, and a bar at one end. A single slot machine sat on the bar. Jack began to feed it quarters.

Amy finished her drink. He made her another one. The phone at the bar rang.

"Your daddy's here," Robert Red said.

As Jack put down the phone, he heard Dexter and Evelyn talking on the stairs. Amy recognized his voice too.

Dexter came into the room. Amy had turned on the barstool to face him.

If Dexter was surprised, he was able to conceal it.

"Didn't know you were a member of this club," Dexter said.

"Robert Red gave me the key," Jack said.

"He's always getting into things out here," Dexter said to Evelyn. "One day I came down here. Found him and Robert Red had taken the slot machine apart and were running change through it to see how long it would take to pay off."

Evelyn laughed.

"I gave him a good whipping for that," Dexter said.

"Hello, Dexter," Amy said.

The words sounded strange coming out of her mouth. Jack remembered how his mother pronounced the name, dropping the *r*. Amy had said it exactly the same way.

"I met Amy in the hospital," Dexter said. "She was doing her nurse training. Had a broken arm from when that damn horse threw me."

Amy laughed.

"All the nurses were scared of you," she said.

"But not you," Dexter said.

"I knew how to handle you," she said.

Jack wondered if the two had practiced this scene for his benefit.

"Make us some drinks, boy," Dexter said.

Jack wanted to hit the old man, to feel his face give way beneath his fist.

"I'll help," Evelyn said.

She took his arm and pulled him toward the bar. She fixed herself a vodka martini and Dexter a straight whiskey.

"You be careful," she whispered. "Remember, she means nothing to him. He still loves Margaret."

"He loves nobody," Jack said.

Jack watched the old man get his way just as he always did. It was as if he took control of everyone's mind the moment he entered a room. Jack felt suffocated, as if the lake had risen and filled the room with water. He drank straight whiskey now, not even tasting it as he swallowed.

Amy and Dexter stood before the jukebox. Amy ran her hands over the glowing glass front.

"Play Elvis," she said. "Not old Johnny Cash or that ugly Willie Nelson."

Dexter dropped change in the jukebox. They heard Elvis singing "Love Me Tender."

"I want to dance," Amy said. "Jack never takes me dancing. I sit out on that barge with Dumas all day and fool with snakes."

Dexter laughed. He did not look like an old man now. He looked young, maybe as young as when he had courted Margaret, his hair slicked back in a pompadour, his teeth perfect and white when he smiled at her. They waltzed smoothly over the dance floor.

"Let's dance too," Evelyn said.

Evelyn was a big woman and her head came almost to Jack's neck. He felt drunk and was worried about where he was going to put his feet. He felt as if he were dancing underwater in the thick mud on the bottom of the lake. The room swayed, the jukebox sending blue and red lights against the black ceiling.

The record was over, and they all went to the bar.

"You get the money?" Dexter asked Amy.

"Wasn't what you promised," she said.

"It's all you're going to get."

"Jack's going to take care of me," Amy said. "By Christmas we'll be rich. I want to buy one of those cars with white leather upholstery. Once I saw Elvis on the street in Memphis. He could have given me a Cadillac."

Jack watched himself sway back and forth in the mirror behind the bar.

"We'll be rich," Amy said. "Won't we, Jack?"

"Jack'll take better care of you than Elvis would've," Dexter said.

Dexter laughed, and Evelyn whispered in his ear. She tried to pull him away from the bar, but he ignored her.

"Better than you have," Jack said.

"Sometimes I wonder if you're really my son," Dexter said.

"By spring I'll be planting my land," Jack said.

Jack stood face-to-face with Dexter.

"Jack," Evelyn said.

He reached out and took hold of Dexter, feeling the hard muscles of the forearm. Not an old man's arm yet.

"Stop," Evelyn said.

Dexter did not move but stood grinning at him.

"That pussy has got you turned inside out," Dexter said.

"Maybe she was yours. Now she's mine," Jack said.

"I don't belong to any man," Amy said from her seat on a barstool.

Evelyn was pulling Dexter away. Jack let him go.

"I don't care about her," Dexter said, pointing at Amy. "I don't care about any of them."

"Am I one too?" Evelyn asked.

"You know what I think of you," Dexter said.

"Both of them are the same," Amy said. "Exactly the same. I could close my eyes in bed and not know which one it was."

"I'm not like him," Jack said.

Dexter said, "Boy, you've got a long way to go before you're a man."

"I understand you, Dexter," Evelyn said. "But sometimes I get so tired of it all. You want a fight with Jack."

"Thinks he can whip me," Dexter said. "He's got a few more years to wait."

"I'm so sick of fighting," Amy said. "Fighting dogs, fighting men."

Evelyn said to Amy, "Honey, come on up to the bar. I'll buy you a drink. They can stay down here and kill each other if they want."

Amy and Evelyn went up the stairs. Jack's scars itched, and he rubbed them through his shirt. Dexter began to feed money into the slot machine. Jack started up the stairs.

"That's what they want," Dexter said. "Us to follow them."

Jack continued up the stairs, listening to the clank of the

machine as Dexter pulled the handle. Dexter was right, but he could not stay in the same room with the old man.

Let him stay by himself, Jack thought. Feeding money in the machine, which was going to beat him in the end. Just as in the end he would have the land and Amy if he wanted her. Dexter would be left with nothing.

Jack heard Dexter pull the handle. Coins jingled in the chute as the machine paid off. Dexter chuckled, and Jack hurried up the stairs.

Chapter Seventeen

They began the harvest in early September. The whole community turned out. Tudor put up drying sheds, frameworks of saplings covered by sheets of plastic to keep off the rain and dew. Over the sheds they draped camouflage netting Blackmon had bought at a war surplus store in Memphis.

Just like artillery emplacements, Jack thought.

But instead of the smell of powder and grease and diesel fuel there was the stink of the drying plants.

Tudor directed the workers as they hung up the plants in the sheds. Tops and side tops were hung on cords stretched across the sheds. The children stripped the leaves and branches, which were placed in wooden cribs to dry. Tudor laid sheets of plastic on the ground to catch any buds or resin that might drop off.

A week later they were finishing the job on a hot afternoon, the sun low over the trees.

Jack's hands were soon covered with sticky resin. Tudor went about the field with a white plastic lard bucket, collecting resin from the hands of the workers. He stopped where Jack and Amy were cutting tops. They rubbed their hands together and picked the tiny balls of resin off them.

Tudor was smoking one of his cigar-sized joints, his little black snake eyes examining their hands for any trace of resin they might have missed.

"This is the good shit," Tudor said, rubbing the resin bits into a marble-sized ball between his palms and then dropping it into the bucket.

"What are you going to do with your share?" Jack asked.

"Buy land," Tudor said. "Send my children to the university. They'll be the doctors and the lawyers. I'll be a farmer like Blackmon or your daddy."

"No money in farming."

"Can hold your head up if you're a big farmer."

Jack wondered what the rest were going to do. Some had talked about moving to Florida. But most of them were planning to stay in Egypt Ridge. Francis wanted to open another store in Greenville.

"I'm going to New York," Amy said. "Don't ever want to see Mississippi again."

Jack was not sure he would give her a dime. He was beginning to believe her when she said she cared for no one but herself.

Blackmon met them at one of the drying sheds when they brought in a load of tops in plastic garbage bags.

"Jaban's here," he said.

Amy turned pale.

"How do you know?" Jack asked.

"I invited him," Blackmon said. "So he'll see what good stuff we're growing. It'll mean more money for us."

Jack went to the tree where he had chained Alligator. Children belonging to Tudor's kin squatted in imitation of their fathers just outside the reach of the chain.

"Mister, is that Mr. Dexter Purse's mean dog?" a boy asked.

"He is," Jack said.

Jack unchained Alligator.

"You ain't afraid of him?" the boy asked.

"I'm afraid," Jack said.

"You put the meanness on him?" the boy asked. "He put his on you?"

"No, he's not my dog," Jack said.

He was glad Amy was not there to hear the boy.

"You're just like that dog," Amy liked to say.

Alligator sniffed at Jack's leg. Jack could smell the dog's stink and wondered what he smelled like to Alligator. Was it a stink or something else?

He brought Alligator to heel. The boys stepped back, and he walked away with the dog.

By the big cottonwood he found Amy talking to Blackmon.

"She's done something," Blackmon said.

Jaban had come by boat. Tudor was bringing him up from the river.

"What did you do?" Blackmon asked.

"Nothing," Amy said.

Blackmon took hold of her arms and shook her.

"Tell me, bitch," Blackmon said.

Amy was crying. Blackmon shook her again, the emerald earrings sparkling in the light. Jack stepped forward to stop Blackmon, holding the chain up tight against Alligator who, excited by the violence, ignored his commands to heel and was pulling hard.

"Tell me," Blackmon hissed, his mouth close to her face. "You'll ruin everything we've worked for."

"It was only a little," she said.

Blackmon let her go. She started to run to Jack but seeing Alligator she stopped. Jack thought she was going to start crying again. Instead she drew herself up tall and straight.

"A little what?" Blackmon said. "Honey, we need to know. That man will be here in five minutes."

"Cocaine," she said.

Blackmon smiled. "I knew damn well this wasn't about love. Good, you can give it back."

"Wasn't much," Amy said. "Did a couple of lines. It's gone."

"It was more than that," Blackmon said.

"Dumas did some too," Amy said. "We'd do a line and go catch snakes."

Blackmon laughed.

"What else did you and that old nigger do out in the woods?" Blackmon asked.

"Shut up," Jack said.

Alligator pulled hard against the chain, the strap cutting into Jack's hands. He made Alligator sit down. He wished he had the muzzle on him.

"Dexter wouldn't have let her make a fool of him," Blackmon said.

Amy laughed.

"Nobody's made a fool of me," Jack said.

"He'll want payment for what she stole," Blackmon said. "Come out of your share."

"All right," Jack said. "But don't put your hands on her again."

"We'll walk out and meet him," Blackmon said. "Make it right."

"I don't want to see him," Amy said.

"Maybe you better," Jack said.

"He won't be wanting money," she said. "Don't let him hurt me."

"He won't touch you," Jack said.

Jack borrowed Evelyn's pistol, telling her he wanted to go shoot snakes.

They walked along the track to the river. When they had gone a few hundred yards, Jack saw Alligator's ears stand up. They walked around a bend, and Jack saw Jaban and Billy Ray flanked by Tudor and one of his cousins. Billy Ray wore a Fila tennis warm-up. Jaban was dressed in khaki pants and a blue work shirt. He could have been a young Memphis lawyer getting ready to mow his lawn.

Tudor carried his shotgun slung over his shoulder with the piece of yellow ski rope.

"I done like you told me," Tudor said to Blackmon. "Made 'em leave their guns at the boat." Tudor pointed a skinny arm at Billy Ray and went on, "Heavy here didn't want to give his up. Had one of them Jew machine guns. I'll take this shotgun over it anytime."

Billy Ray laughed, curling his lips back from his teeth.

"Swamp rat like you wouldn't last a minute against an Uzi," Billy Ray said. "That gun of yours a muzzle loader?"

Jaban touched Billy Ray on the arm.

"Later," Jaban said.

Billy Ray shrugged his shoulders and shut up.

"She told me what she did," Blackmon said to Jaban. "We want to make it right."

"Let me have her," Jaban said.

Amy stepped close to Jack. He put his arm around her.

Jaban said, "When she left, a kilo of coke went with her."

Blackmon turned to look at Amy.

"Damn you," Blackmon said.

"Deal's off unless you hand her over," Jaban said. "And don't try to distribute it in Memphis on your own."

"We don't need you," Jack said.

"Think what Dexter would do," Blackmon pleaded. "He wouldn't lose it all over a woman."

Jack cocked the .357 and held it on Jaban.

"If you're not out of here in ten seconds, I'm going to blow your head off," Jack said.

Amy ran a little way back up the track and stopped.

He began to count. Jaban stood smiling. By the time he reached six, Billy Ray was tugging at Jaban's arm.

"Come on, come on," Billy Ray said. "These are crazy people."

Jaban backed away. Jack stood and watched them until they disappeared around the bend in the track.

"You figure out a way to sell the crop," Blackmon said.

Blackmon walked off toward the field, followed by Tudor and the cousin.

Jack looked at Amy. She stood in the dusty track, holding herself stiff as if she were a mannequin set there by someone as a joke.

"Take the dog back to the field," Jack said. "Chain him to a tree."

"No, he'll bite me," Amy said.

"He won't," Jack said. "I want to follow them. Make sure they leave."

"No," she said.

"Maybe I should call Jaban back."

Jack hated her now, believed everything she had ever told him about not trusting her.

Amy took hold of the chain. He brought Alligator to heel.

"You'd like it if this dog killed me," she said. "He'll do what you're afraid to do yourself. Well, I'm not afraid of either one of you."

They walked off together, Amy holding the extreme end of the chain, letting the middle drag in the dust.

"Don't you let him get loose," Jack called after her. "That's a valuable animal."

She did not reply or turn her head at the sound of his voice, just kept walking, the chain kicking up little puffs of dust.

He cut through the woods and made his way to the riverbank through a cane thicket. They had come down from Memphis in a cabin cruiser, now anchored in a big eddy below the sandbar. Jaban was at the wheel, the engine idling. Another man was pulling up an anchor. He did not see Billy Ray and guessed he was below. The boat swung out into the current and started upriver, the Arkansas side already in darkness.

Jack had just started back through the woods when he heard a yell and a single shot. More shouts followed as he ran toward the sound.

Billy Ray was up a tree he had climbed while being pursued by Alligator. His Ruger assault carbine was on the ground. But Alligator had gone right up after him, probably using the same low limb to pull himself up on that Billy Ray had. Now Alligator had pushed the man out on the end of a long limb. The limb creaked as

Billy Ray shifted his weight. Jack expected it to break if Alligator forced him further out on it. The dog was only a few feet away and was picking his way cautiously along the limb, the chain dangling. Jack was afraid if Alligator fell he would hang himself.

"Get him away!" Billy Ray shouted. "He's gone crazy. What's he doing up a tree?"

"Can climb a tree better than a fox," Jack said.

"Call him off," Billy Ray pleaded.

Part of one leg of Billy Ray's warm-up was gone. He was bleeding from a long gash on his calf. Alligator had probably hooked an eyetooth there, but Billy Ray had been strong enough to pull away before the dog could find a good hold.

"Got you treed just like a coon," Jack said. "Why aren't you on the boat?"

"Call him down," Billy Ray said.

"I want to know," Jack said.

Billy Ray moved further out on the limb, which suddenly gave a sharp crack, like a rifle shot.

"Jaban is crazy over that girl," Billy Ray said, talking fast. "Was going to marry her. Gave her a ring. Then she stole the coke and ran off. Sent me to follow you and find out where she's staying. Please, call him off."

Jack called Alligator down out of the tree. The dog sat on his haunches and looked up at Billy Ray, who now stood on a large limb, one arm around the trunk of the tree.

"Come on down," Jack said.

Billy Ray said, "Not while that dog's loose."

Jack unloaded the carbine, tossing the magazine into the bushes.

"Tell Jaban to stay away from this island," Jack said.

"I'll tell him," Billy Ray said. "Tie up that dog."

"Tell Jaban I'll pay for the coke," Jack said.

"He wants her, not money," Billy Ray said. "Can't let it get out that people can steal from him."

"Tell him to forget about her," Jack said.

Jack put Alligator on his belt and walked away from the tree. He tossed the carbine into the first creek they passed.

He found Amy eating a watermelon with some of the children. They were having a seed-spitting contest.

"I'm sorry," she said. "He was going to bite me. So I let him go."

A boy gave her a set of watermelon teeth he had carved out of the rind. Amy put them in her mouth and pretended she was a vampire. The children screamed and laughed as she chased them outside the circle of lantern light into the growing darkness.

"Lucky for you nothing happened to him," Jack said.

"I told you I couldn't handle him," she said. "Nobody ever believes what I say."

Jack thought of her and Dumas getting coked out of their minds and hunting snakes. Dexter had been right about Amy. Now he was stuck with her.

"Got any of it left?" he asked.

"No, we used it all," she said. "There was never a kilo. A few grams. That's all."

"You can't be trusted."

"I've told you that enough times. Don't let him give me to Billy Ray. Billy Ray likes to cut girls."

Jack thought he should have left Billy Ray to Alligator or killed him himself. Next time might not be so easy.

It was clear Blackmon had told no one what had happened with Jaban. They finished the harvest by lantern light, the lanterns moving among the plants like huge fireflies. People began to gather around the table filled with food.

The women held a marijuana cooking contest to celebrate the last day of the harvest. The entries were laid out on a long table, waiting to be judged: barbecued ribs covered with a marijuana sauce, rhubarb pie, greens, fried catfish, apple cobbler, fried green tomatoes, candied yams, and peach ice cream. The centerpiece of the table was a model and architect's drawing of Bascomb Dodd's new church.

"Let's eat," Amy said.

She led him to the table where he began to sample Francis's sister's potato salad and some of Sally Ann's chicken. He wanted to get high with the rest of them and not have to think about how they were going to market the crop.

"You got it figured out yet?" Blackmon asked.

"I'll think of a way," he said.

"It would have been so easy. Damn girl screwed it up," Blackmon said.

The judges awarded the prize to an okra and tomato dish made by Travis's cousin. By now everyone was stoned. People gathered around the table and ate everything in sight. Wade and Norris were eating peach ice cream with their hands and laughing.

"I warned you," Amy said, standing close and wrapping her arms around him. "I told you I'd do crazy things."

"Get away from me," he said.

He wanted to enjoy the mood the high had created within him.

"You like to hurt," she said. "Just like your daddy."

She turned her back on him and went to play with the children.

Jack found Tudor and explained to him about Billy Ray. They left the field and went into the woods to guard against the return of Jaban. His scars itched, and he rubbed them through his shirt, thinking that this was like leaving base camp to set up a night ambush as the sound of his neighbors' talk and laughter beneath the lantern light faded behind him to be replaced by darkness and the hum of insects.

Chapter Eighteen

Jack looked down at Tudor's cousin: the thin unshaven face, eyes wide open, the mouth a dark hole. The man lay on the sand, the flies buzzing about him, the river sliding by thick and brown a few feet away. His green T-shirt was filled with holes. Blackmon examined the body, brushing away the flies.

"Machine gun," Blackmon said.

Tudor took off his shirt and draped it over the face, ignoring the flies that lighted on his sunken, hairless chest.

"Big man done it," Tudor said, squatting by the body and touching one of the holes. "Done it with that Jew gun."

Tudor brushed the flies away from the body.

"Came down the river in a boat," Tudor said. "Lonnie never knew who they were until it was too late. Never got a chance to shoot back."

"Take that girl back to Jaban," Blackmon said. "Make it right."

"You don't know it was Billy Ray," Jack said.

"Big man done it," Tudor said, pointing at the holes in Lonnie's chest. "Only one kind of gun can do that."

Blackmon said, "Jack, you fix it. He'll kill all of us if you don't."

The next day a black tractor driver was found in his truck riddled with bullets. Blackmon called a meeting on the riverboat.

"It's all over that woman," Travis said. "She's got to go."

"Take her back," Wade said.

"You can't do that," Evelyn said. "He'll kill her."

"So we should let them kill all of us," Norris said. "Put her out

157

on the road. Whatever happens won't be our fault. They'll kill all of us."

Norris looked as if he were about to cry. Jack felt the same, his chance to regain the land slipping away from him.

"I'll take care of Jaban," Jack said.

"You can't do it," Norris said. "They got machine guns."

Norris pulled at his hair as he paced about the pilothouse.

Evelyn said, "Be still, Norris. Always tugging at your hair. When your mama took away that sugar tit, you started tugging."

Everyone laughed.

"Jack can do it," Evelyn said.

"I want the big man," Tudor said.

"No use going up there unless you get Jaban," Wade said. "Get anybody else, and it'll just make him mad."

"I'll go too," Robert Red said. "I've been all over his farm."

Jack made a model of the house and grounds, using his and Robert Red's knowledge of the place. Robert Red wanted to fly up and take pictures, but Jack felt that was too risky. Besides, more people from Egypt Ridge might die while they were doing recon. He had them rehearse their approach to the house over and over until Tudor got mad and said it was worse than school.

"I want to kill them, not them kill us," Jack said.

He wanted to use Blackmon's house for a practice run but decided they could not afford to take the time. Everyone in the community was carrying guns. Sally Ann had come close to shooting Norris when he came home late one night after slipping out of the house without telling her. She was getting ready to cut him in half with a shotgun when he stepped on Norris Junior's skateboard in the dark and went down cussing and she recognized his voice.

They drove up in Jack's truck. Tudor had his shotgun, Robert Red a Belgian-made machine-gun pistol that Bugger had taken off a German, and Jack a .44 that Evelyn had lent him. Tudor rode between them, smelling of fish. He insisted on smoking a joint, but Jack made him throw it out when they drove out of the county.

"You'll be too fucked up to do any shooting," Jack told him.

"Leave the big man to me," Tudor said.

Jack looked at his little black snake eyes, which never seemed to blink, and believed that stoned or straight Tudor was going to waste Billy Ray.

At the farm they hid the truck in some trees off a gravel road about a mile from the house. They waited for dark.

"They probably got guards," Robert Red said as he took the wooden stock on and off the machine-gun pistol.

"Won't be expecting us," Jack said. "Done this a hundred times in 'Nam. Going to be easy."

Tudor grinned foolishly and said, "Easy."

"Look at him," Robert Red said. "He's fucking stoned."

"Easy, easy," Tudor cooed.

"Just do what I tell you," Jack said. "You'll be all right."

Jack kept telling himself this was not going to be any different than Vietnam. But it was. All he had to do was get in the truck and drive away. In the war he never had any choice. Yet there was really no choice here. Jaban was going to keep killing them one by one, his friends and neighbors. Too late to get out and run now.

Robert Red went to sleep on the front seat of the truck and Tudor on the ground, curled up like one of his coonhounds.

Jack sat on the hood and stood watch. Beyond them the trees were sparse, the ground covered with short grass. And he thought of going to his mother's park with her every Sunday while everyone else was in church. She had stopped going to church, not long after he had found out about the woman in Greenville. Bascomb had come out to the house to talk with her. But he came only that one time and never again. What had they talked about? He remembered Dexter had laughed about Bascomb's visit, and his mother had gotten angry.

Instead of church they went to the park, leaving Dexter at home. She liked to fish for catfish. They used chicken livers for bait and spinning rods, fishing a deep pool below a stretch of shallow water that had been a shoals before the Corps of Engineers had deepened the channel.

They fished until noon, when they returned to the arbor for lunch. Sometimes instead of fishing he cut the grass or made repairs on the arbor. Lunch was always the same: fried chicken, potato salad, and peach cobbler. But she was a terrible cook, the chicken soggy, the potato salad too dry, and the cobbler either too sweet or burned on the bottom. Usually he was so hungry that he did not notice, his hands smelling of chicken livers, catfish, and the river.

Between them was an unspoken rule that they were not to speak of Dexter. Usually they talked about the fish they had caught or those that had been caught in the past.

"When I was a girl, they caught one as long as a man," she said.

And he, "No more of those."

"They are still there," she said, pointing out at the river. "Down deep on the bottom of the channel."

She spoke the words in a hushed tone as if she were speaking of God hiding on the bottom of the river instead of catfish.

He remembered those Sundays as if every one of them were a blue-sky day filled with sunshine. Why had she cut him off? Their only link a collection of postcards from around the world and Christmas presents. Now there were only the cards, perhaps one a year, all written in a backward-slanting spidery hand.

Around midnight he woke them.

"Once the shooting starts, kill anything that moves," Jack said. "Wade won't be able to protect us here. We can't leave witnesses. Nobody there but Jaban's men and whores."

"I ain't shooting women," Tudor said.

"Somebody identifies you and you'll be up on murder charges," Robert Red said.

"No killing women," Tudor said.

"Then make sure you get Billy Ray," Jack said. "He gets a chance to use that Uzi and we're all dead."

They put on gloves. Jack wore a pair of pigskin shooting gloves that belonged to Dexter. Tudor put on a pair of pink rubber dish-washing gloves. Jack and Robert Red laughed.

"When the killing time comes, we'll see who does the best," Tudor said.

They walked through the trees and into an open pasture. A cow lowed in the distance. Lights were on next to the house, lots of them.

"Somebody forgot to turn off the tennis court lights," Jack said.

They followed Robert Red across the pasture and down into a dry creekbed. Robert Red had told them they could walk almost to the house without being seen.

Tudor stopped, pointing at the ground.

"There's a wire," he whispered in Jack's ear.

Tudor wanted to disarm the booby trap and continue, but Jack decided against it, arguing it was too risky because there were probably more of them.

They decided to come out of the creek and retraced their steps to a place where the cattle had come down for water before the pool had dried up, the ground all rutted from their tracks.

Jack led them across the pasture, and they slipped under the barbed-wire fence. He was not scared as he had been on night ambushes during the war. But he felt disgust at what he was getting ready to do. Then he thought of Tudor's cousin and the black tractor driver Dwain Bell. He had seen him before on Blackmon's place, in the air-conditioned cab of one of the big tractors, his head bobbing to the sound of the music from the tape deck. Jaban would kill them all if he did nothing.

He sent Robert Red to the front door and Tudor to the back. They had ten minutes to reach their positions and in another five minutes, or at the sound of the first shot, they were to enter the house. He was going to approach across the patio. As he crawled past where the tennis court lights spilled out onto the field, he saw someone lying on the ground. He froze, wondering if he had been seen, but the figure was in the light and he was in the dark so he was probably safe. Whoever it was, he was going to have to dispose

of him quickly and quietly. In a few minutes Tudor and Robert Red
would enter the house. He took out his skinning knife and keeping
in the darkness crawled toward the figure. When he was twenty
yards away, he realized the man was asleep or drunk, because he
was lying with his arm folded under him at an awkward angle.

Ten yards from the man and getting ready to rush forward and
slit his throat, he realized the man was dead. And not ten yards
away was a dog, lying still on the grass. He reached the man and
turned him over, the body not yet stiff but having that rubbery,
heavy, cold feel of the freshly killed. The pit bull was riddled with
bullets.

On the tennis court he found Jaban with a single bullet hole in
the head. Whoever had done the killing was an expert, probably a
team of men, but they had not counted on finding Lester's pit bull
and had wasted time and ammunition on the dog. He went up
across the patio, the door to the house standing open. In the
kitchen a girl lay slumped across the table, again the victim of a
single well-placed shot.

Jack pushed open the door leading out of the kitchen and took a
step into the darkened room, feeling on the wall with his hand for
the light switch. He heard the dog before he saw it, and then the
dog was in the air, and he shot, not really seeing him but holding on
a piece of denser darkness. The sound of the gun filled up the
room. The recoil whipped the muzzle up, and he pulled it down to
put another round in the head of the dog at his feet. When he
turned the lights on, he found he had killed a big brindled pit bull.

The machine-gun pistol chattered from the living room. Jack ran
into the room to find Robert standing with his back against the
wall, holding the machine-gun pistol with both hands. Two dead
pit bulls lay bleeding on the carpet.

"Opened a door, and they came at me," Robert Red said. "Let's
get out of here. There's dead people and dead dogs all over this
house."

Jack told him about Jaban, and they went to look for Tudor. His
job had been to secure the second floor. In an upstairs bedroom

they found Billy Ray, shot in his bed, a dead girl beside him, but not Tudor. Then in the back of the house they heard the sound of a Jacuzzi. When they walked into the room, they saw Tudor sitting in it amid a mound of soap bubbles and smoking a huge joint. Still wearing his pink gloves, he was fingering the Uzi.

"Ain't had me a good bath in a while," Tudor said. "Best tub I've ever seen. Big man was clean. Now he's dead. Big shots got themselves a professional job done on them. Glad I didn't have to kill no women."

They got him out of the Jacuzzi. Tudor smelled of soap with just a trace of the fish smell beneath it.

As they drove toward home, Jack kept expecting the blue light to come on at any moment. But when they reached Memphis and nobody had stopped them, they all took a hit off Tudor's joint before throwing it out of the car for the drive through the city.

Jack drove down into the Delta, the road straight, and here and there clusters of lights that marked houses, separated by immense stretches of darkness that were the fields.

At Egypt Ridge they drove out to the river.

"Daddy was proud of this gun," Robert Red said as he wiped it clean with a rag.

"Should've carried a shotgun," Tudor said. "I get to keep my gun. Hope I never get important enough to get shot in the head with a twenty-two pistol. They were just like a bunch of pigs at slaughter time."

Robert Red threw the gun far out into the river, it making a sharp chunk when it hit. Jack followed with the .44.

They drove back across the levee and through the fields to home. He felt like stopping the car and walking the dark fields, the land that was soon going to be his. He wanted to kneel down and dig his hands deep into the warm black soil that by spring would be covered with his cotton and beans.

Chapter Nineteen

Blackmon announced at a meeting on the riverboat he had found a new buyer for the crop in New Orleans. All they had to do was take it to a pickup point between Baton Rouge and New Orleans. There the buyer had set up a temporary warehouse where the crop would be stored until it could be graded and a price fixed. Then it would be loaded on trucks and distributed all over the country.

The crop was dry and ready to ship. They packed the tops and plants into thirty-pound bales, which they wrapped in plastic. Some wanted to take it down by truck, but Blackmon argued for a trip by river on the *Nathan B.*

"We'll have to hire a pilot and an engineer," Wade said.

"Yeah, by the time we're through the whole state of Mississippi will own a share in this crop," Norris said.

"I was thinking of Toby Morris," Blackmon said.

"Didn't they take away his pilot's license?" Evelyn asked.

"No, got fired for drinking," Wade said.

"I can be his engineer," Robert Red said.

Everyone agreed that Robert Red could handle the engines. He pulled his own maintenance on his airplane.

"We should rent trucks," Norris said.

Blackmon said, "It'll take two, maybe three tractor trailer rigs. Folks'll ask questions about us renting trucks. Boat already belongs to us."

"We're going to get caught," Norris said. "Trucks are safer."

"We'll be a wedding party," Evelyn said. "We can say we chartered the boat for a wedding and a trip to New Orleans."

"See, Norris?" Jack said. "Nobody'll be suspicious of that."

Norris was not convinced and continued to complain as they left the boat.

When Dexter found out, he made Blackmon pay him for his share of the boat. Blackmon offered to pay him more out of the profits, but Dexter demanded the money before the trip started.

Everyone liked the idea of the riverboat wedding. The women bought dresses in Greenville and Memphis just as if an actual wedding were to take place. They ordered a cake and cases of champagne. Norris pointed out they had better keep the champagne away from Toby or the boat and its cargo were going to end up on the bottom of the river.

The ladies chose Amy as the bride. She was excited about it. She fussed over the choice of a dress. Jack agreed reluctantly to stand in as the groom.

"You make a handsome couple," Evelyn kept saying.

And when Dexter heard about it he laughed and said, "Be careful, boy. Bascomb'll marry you and make it stick."

Jack planned on taking Alligator with him because Dexter was going to Texas to meet with some dog men about the fight, which was only a month away.

They left the lake early in the morning with Toby Morris at the wheel. He pulled on ropes that rang bells in the engine room and addressed his engineer through the speaking tube as Mr. Red. Toby chewed tobacco, from time to time aiming a brown stream into one of the twin brass spittoons on either side of the wheel. He looked sober to Jack, but they had all agreed to watch him closely and keep him out of the champagne, which had been iced down in washtubs.

Bascomb Dodd had brought along the model of his church,

which was on display on a table in the dining room. Children dressed in their Sunday clothes ran around the boat. Some of the women were busy in the galley cooking dinner. Two children shucked corn at the rail and threw the husks into the river, white silk and green husks floating on the brown water. Travis was there with some of the blacks to make sure they got their share of the money upon delivery. Everyone was talking about what they were going to do with the money that would be theirs in a few days. They had stored bales in the galley, the cabins, and even in the pilothouse to keep them off the deck. But they ran out of room and had to put some there, which they covered with tarps.

They left the lake and entered the river. Bascomb called everyone together in the dining room.

"I'm in a marrying mood," Bascomb Dodd said. "Too bad it won't be the real thing. We'll go through it just like it's a rehearsal."

Jack had Alligator on the chain.

"Get somebody else," he said. "I have to mind this dog."

He started to go back to the pilothouse.

"It won't hurt," Amy said. "Please. Chain him up."

Jack thought she looked beautiful in the wedding gown, all lace and silk, that Sally Ann's sister had been married in. Amy had insisted on wearing her emerald earrings. He was uncomfortable in the dinner jacket he had rented in Memphis.

They all clamored at him. If Alligator had not been at his feet, he thought the little flower girls would have taken him by the hands and pulled him to where Bascomb was standing, Bible in hand. Instead they kept their distance, watched by Alligator.

Evelyn shooed the girls away and said, "People have gone to all this trouble. They want to see a wedding even if it's a pretend one."

So Jack went through the ceremony with Amy, ending up with a ring on his finger and rice in his hair. They opened the champagne. Only Tudor, still dressed in his khaki swamper's clothes, was smoking a joint as he watched Alligator, whose chain Jack had made fast to the rail, dog and man surrounded by a semicircle of small boys. Now that the crop was sold the people seemed to have lost interest in marijuana. Most were getting very drunk on the champagne. Smoking marijuana had been a temporary thing with them, and now that the crop was about to be sold they wanted to return to the old ways of doing things. Bascomb Dodd would preach no more sermons about the virtues of getting stoned. Everyone had done plenty of sinning lately, and Jack guessed the first few sermons would be good ones. Bascomb wanted the people in his new church acting the same way their fathers and grandfathers had. Evelyn took pictures of Amy and Jack cutting the cake, and the fake wedding was over.

Jack and Amy went up on the hurricane deck, standing among the hog chains and hog chain braces. Toby had the glass windows of the pilothouse open, the boat vibrating with the throb of the diesel engines, the paddle wheel churning the river, beating the brown water into a white foam. The smell of diesel fuel mixed with the moldy river smell and Amy's perfume.

"We could do it for real when we get back," Jack said.

Amy did not answer, but he was sure she had heard what he had said. She looked off toward the big timber on the Arkansas side.

"It was a pretty wedding," she said.

His scars itched. It was hot out on the deck despite the breeze. He looked to the pilothouse and saw Toby and Blackmon arguing over a bottle of champagne. Blackmon threw it into the river, the bottle sparkling in the sunlight as it fell in an arc toward the brown water.

"I told you about me," she said. "You could have been killed or gone to jail over Jaban. I'd just do something like that to you."

"You want everything to fail," he said. "Turn to shit."

"I know it's going to," she said. Then she paused and shaded her eyes with her hand against the sun. "It's so hot. Not a spot of shade up here."

She unbuttoned the top of her dress. She had already taken off her veil, her long hair blowing in the breeze. Jack thought it was as if he were watching a snake shed its skin. The white lace on the dress had that same brittle geometrical texture to it. The fabric rustled under her fingers.

"Dexter understood me," she said. "You don't."

"You must enjoy being treated like a whore."

"He was nice to me. Treated me like a lady. You could take lessons from him."

Jack thought of Jaban and Billy Ray. He was glad they were dead. Both of them deserved killing. But he was angry he had been maneuvered into going up there. If they had arrived an hour earlier, they would have run into the professional killers.

"Goddamn, I've been nice to you!" Jack said. "Plenty of people wanted to turn you over to Jaban."

"I can't be your sweet wife," she said. "I can't stay home and cook. Put up vegetables out of the garden. Teach Sunday school. That's what you want."

The heat radiated off the metal deck, the surface hard under Jack's thin dress shoes.

"You can do anything you want," he said.

"In Egypt Ridge?" she asked. "Let's take the money and go to Mexico. Live in one of those hotels right on the beach."

"I want the land," he said. "Money'll be gone in a few years."

"Put it in the stock market," she said. "We could have a good time in Mexico."

"You'd marry me?"

"No, but I'd live with you."

"The land won't go away. It'll always be there."

"For some bank to own after you go bankrupt. You'll spend all your time on that land, breaking your back. No time to pay any mind to me."

"Jack," Tudor called from the passenger deck. "Come get this dog."

"That dog and dirt. That's all you care about," she said.

He left her there, standing amid the heat waves rising off the metal, in the white dress, the green earrings flashing in the light, and went down to where Alligator lay panting in the shade by the rail.

They kept Toby sober by watching him day and night. But just above Vicksburg, Robert Red began to have trouble with the engines. A rocker arm had broken and new bearings were needed. They put into the port for repairs, the town perched on the bluff above them. A Coast Guard cutter was tied up at the wharf, and Jack hoped they were not going to get caught after coming this far. Norris was frantic. He wanted to leave and go back home. Blackmon and Wade, at the request of Sally Ann, locked him in a cabin.

"Remember, you're a wedding party on your way to New Orleans to have a good time. Go into town. Spend some money in the stores. Act like tourists," Blackmon told them.

Jack spent the day with Alligator and Evelyn touring the battlefield. From Confederate artillery positions at the top of the bluff they could see the riverboat tied up at the wharf. Amy had gone off by herself, saying she was going to find an air-conditioned bar and have herself a mixed drink. He hoped that Robert Red had been able to find a machine shop that could make a new rocker arm for the ancient diesel. Meanwhile Robert Red and Tudor were repacking the bearings.

By suppertime Norris had calmed down enough to be released from his cabin. Sally Ann returned from shopping.

"She paid a hundred dollars for a brass lizard," Norris said. "Haven't made a dime off the crop and she's spending it already. Thing was made in Taiwan."

Shortly after midnight, as he lay in his berth in his cabin, Jack heard the engines start. It was still hot and uncomfortable in the cabin, which was filled with the stink of the dog and the locker room smell of his own sweat. Bales were stacked in the other berth and piled high along one wall.

The door swung open. It was Amy. For a moment she hesitated when she saw the dog. Alligator raised his ears and stood up.

"Lie quiet, dog," Jack said.

Alligator sat down, still watching Amy.

"I was mean to you," she said.

He guessed she was a little drunk. Then he looked at her eyes, noticed the dilated pupils, and decided she was stoned.

"Talk sweet to me again," she said.

"What are you on?" he asked.

She put her arms around him.

"Say it," she said.

"You have my heart," he said, wondering if it was still true.

"That's so sweet," she said. "Put the dog out. Please."

"He stays. Can't take a chance on anything happening to him."

She took off her clothes until the only thing she was wearing was the emerald earrings. He felt an ache for her. She was like a spring morning in the Delta, the birds singing their hearts out, the fields steaming in the heat from the just-risen sun. He reached out and pulled her down on the bed, rolling on top of her.

Amy wrapped her arms and legs around him in what he knew could be either real or feigned passion, but he did not care. Suddenly she screamed.

"He licked me," she said.

Alligator stood next to the bed.

"Be still," he said.

Carefully he rolled off her, speaking softly and caressingly to the dog as he reached out for his collar. Just as he got his fingers around it, Alligator lunged for her. She pressed herself flat against the wall and began to cry.

"You'll always love me, won't you?" she said.

Jack started to say yes but suddenly realized this was not Amy talking to him. Something was wrong.

"What have you done?" he asked.

"Nothing. Just want you to love me," she said.

"Tell me."

He relaxed his grip on the dog, who had been straining to get at her. Alligator lunged for her, his claws tearing at the sheets.

"I love you," she said.

Alligator had his belly on the bed now. Jack was afraid he was not going to be able to control the dog, whose eyes were beginning to glaze over.

"Tell me now!" he said.

Alligator's jaws clicked as he twisted his head to free himself of the collar.

"The police—I told—get him away!" she said, her eyes wide with terror.

Jack had to use all of his strength to pull the dog off the bed. He got the chain on him and dragged him out of the cabin. He chained him to a steel stair rail and had Tudor stand guard over him.

She was still crying when he returned to the room and refused to talk until he threatened to bring Alligator back. She told him she had had a little of the cocaine left and had been caught doing a line in the ladies' room of a bar by an undercover female narcotics officer. They had threatened her with prison so she had traded information about the boatload of marijuana for immunity from prosecution. Hoping to catch the distributor, the narcotics officers had let her return to the boat.

Jack felt sick. Men had died. He had killed. Now they had failed. If he did not do something quick, they were all going to jail. That meant getting the cargo off the boat. But worst of all was going to be when he had to face Dexter and explain it all.

"What are you going to do?" she asked.

"Don't know. Hide the shit downriver someplace," he said. "Keep your mouth shut. Blackmon or Tudor find out and they'll kill you. Nothing I can do to stop them."

"They were going to send me to prison," she said. "Five years."

"That's not long," Jack said. "You could have done that."

"Don't have time for jail," Amy said. "I'd be an old woman by the time I got out."

He wrapped his arms around her and she cried. Amy being anything but hard as nails made him nervous. So when she knelt down and took him in her mouth, he was relieved. But he could not enjoy the blowjob because every time he tried to close his eyes and relax, Dexter's grinning face appeared before him along with an immense field stretching away to a distant treeline, land that would now never be his.

Chapter Twenty

J
ack watched the people wave to boats they met on the river, not knowing that any one of them could be the narcotics officers. He was even suspicious of the occasional small plane that flew overhead. They could be tracking them from the air. Amy had stayed in her cabin all day, refusing to open the door when he knocked.

Near dusk they tied up below an island not far downriver from Natchez so Toby could get some sleep. People went ashore and built a fire. Children were cooking hot dogs and toasting marshmallows over it.

Jack took Alligator for a run down the sandbar along one side of the island. The channel ran on the Arkansas side so there was no boat traffic, the river sliding by wide and empty, the water glittering in the light of the setting sun. He put the dog on the chain and started back. The light was off the water, blocked by the timber behind him, only a single strip near the shore still lit. Then that was gone. He wished he could stay hidden in the darkness and not have to go back to the boat and tell Blackmon that Amy had sold them out.

Alligator smelled her before he saw her, the dog stopping and sniffing the air. He tugged on the chain, and Jack made him sit down. Amy stood by the water, the pale oval of her face turned toward them, her tennis shoes tied together and hung around her neck. She stepped into the river.

"Wait," he yelled.

He ran toward her, still holding the chain, and the dog quickly outdistanced him so he both ran and was pulled by Alligator to the edge of the water. Alligator sniffed at the prints of her bare feet left in the wet sand. He saw the flash of her hair and heard the steady splash of the slow crawl that he knew she could swim for miles, the current taking her, and gradually the sound was gone. Alligator may have still heard her or smelled her because he pulled hard against the chain, his ears raised.

For a long time Jack stood in the darkness, smelling the river and the stink of Alligator. It was now so dark he could not see the river, only heard the hiss of the water against the sandbar. He could make out the dark mass of timber on the far shore against the lighter sky and hoped Amy had reached it. Alligator tugged on the chain, and he started back for the boat, the mooring marked by the reflection of the fire against the treetops.

Jack told Blackmon what Amy had done. They were alone in the pilothouse. Jack had Alligator on the chain.

"I'll kill her," Blackmon said.

"Too late. She's off on the Mississippi side somewhere," Jack said. "It could have happened to anyone. She was afraid of jail."

"We all need to be afraid of jail," Blackmon said.

Blackmon looked old and worn out, like Jack's company commander after he had learned on the radio an entire platoon had been wiped out in a clever ambush by the NVA.

"What am I going to tell all these people?" Blackmon went on. "We were so close. Just a few days from New Orleans. Help me tell them, Jack."

"They won't want to listen to me," Jack said. He rubbed his scars through his shirt.

"Wasn't your fault," Blackmon said. "She fooled all of us."

"What should we do?" Jack asked.

"Get rid of the cargo," Blackmon said. "Throw it in the river. Burn it. Got to be careful. They could be watching us right now. But maybe not. Maybe they know we've tied up for the night. No need to keep that close on us."

Blackmon gathered everyone together and told them about Amy.

"We're all going to jail," Norris groaned. "I'm getting off this boat."

"Be a man," Sally Ann said, grabbing him by the arm. "Running won't do any good."

"Leave the woman to me," Tudor said.

Tudor had his shotgun slung over his shoulder.

"Nobody's going to do anything about her," Jack said.

"You then," Tudor said. "She has to pay."

Evelyn said, "Stop it! No more killing."

Bascomb stood up and started to lead everyone in a prayer.

"Brothers and sisters—," he began.

"Shut up, preacher," Wade said. "Praying's not going to do any good now. Unless you can pray the cargo off the boat."

"You white folks got fancy lawyers," Travis said. "What's going to happen to us?"

"Nothing's going to happen," Blackmon said. "We just dump the cargo. No evidence. Right, Norris?"

"Yeah, but what if they're watching us right now?" Norris said.

"My guess is that they got a boat on the river but not too close. Scared of spooking us," Blackmon said.

"Throw it in the river," Wade said.

"Bales'll float," Evelyn said.

"Burn it," Travis said.

"You burn it," Norris said. "I'm taking the launch and going over to the Mississippi side. I've got friends in Natchez. They'll take me in. Can't prove I was ever here."

"Nobody leaves," Blackmon said. "Once we burn it we go on to New Orleans just like we planned. They'll stop us sooner or later, but when they search the boat, they won't find anything. It'll be that coke-head's word against ours."

The unloading began. It was well past midnight and most of the children had gone to sleep. They doused the fire and turned all the lights on the boat off. People kept coming up to Jack and telling him how sorry they were about Amy. Jack would have felt better if they had cursed him.

They took the bales off and built three separate pyramids of them on the sandbar, making sure they were stacked loosely with plenty of air space so they would burn quickly. After they doused the pyramids with diesel fuel, they set them afire. Nobody made a sound as they watched months of work go up in flames. The flames singed the leaves of the trees, sparks drifting high into the dark sky.

As the pyramids collapsed, Tudor and others poked at the burning bales with long poles to break them apart and make them burn faster. Everywhere there was the sweet stink of the burning plants. Tudor stood close to the fire, taking deep breaths of smoke into his lungs. His little black eyes glittered in the light from the fire, his pale face red and scorched by the heat. But no one was getting high with Tudor. The others did their best to avoid the smoke. Jack expected the narcotics officers to show up at any moment. But no one appeared on the river: no lights, no boats.

Bascomb Dodd appeared out of the darkness carrying the model of his new church. For a moment Jack thought Bascomb was going to walk into the fire with it, but he stopped right on the edge, his eyes half closed against the heat, and tossed the model into the fire. Then he sank to his knees on the sand and began to cry.

"Too late to cry now, preacher," Tudor said, poking at what was left of the model with his pole.

"My church," Bascomb said.

"Ain't this church enough for you?" Tudor said, pointing up at the dark sky with his pole, the tip ablaze.

Bascomb got up and stalked off into the darkness.

Jack helped Tudor and the others tend the fire. They threw more diesel fuel on the burning bales from time to time. When the morning star rose above the river, there was nothing left but hot ashes. These they shoveled into the water along with bits of plastic wrapping that had somehow escaped the fire.

"We're safe now," Evelyn said.

"Nothing to show for all that work," Jack said.

"It's all up to Alligator now," Evelyn said.

Alligator was asleep next to the tree where Jack had chained him.

"Get that dog killed is all he's going to do," Jack said. "We just burned up millions. Dog'll never be worth that much."

"Dexter knows what he's doing," she said.

Jack said, "Not this time. Same thing happened to us is going to happen to him. Be left with a dead dog and nothing else. Texas Firecracker is too big even for Alligator. Won't be able to toss him in the air."

"Trust your father," Evelyn said.

She put her arm around him.

"Do you trust him?" Jack asked.

Evelyn said, "I love him."

"So did Mother and look what happened to her," Jack said.

Evelyn started to speak but stopped. Then she said, "Talk to Dexter about Margaret."

"I've done talking with him," Jack said.

"I'm sick of your whining," she said. "She didn't want to marry Dexter. Warned him. Always flew from one man to another like a butterfly in a flower garden."

"You wanted him for yourself."

Evelyn held her arms straight down at her sides and clenched her fists. Jack was glad she was not wearing a pistol.

"If I was Dexter, I would have kicked you off the place years ago," Evelyn said.

"Neither one of you has got a farm now," Jack said.

"I'm not wasting any more of my time on you."

"You learned the piece the old man taught you good."

Alligator got up and shook himself, rattling the chain. Jack walked over to take him back to the boat.

The sky lightened over the Mississippi side, patches of fog clinging low over the water. The stars faded and were gone. Robert

Red had started the engines. Men stood by to cast off the mooring lines.

Jack saw Tudor pulling a driftwood log across the sandbar. Once he reached the water, he took off his clothes and tied them in a bundle to the log with his belt and looped the ski rope sling of the shotgun over a branch. His body was as white as the sand. He pushed the log out into the current and swam for the Mississippi shore, his wet head glistening in the light from the rising sun. Soon he was a hundred yards out, swimming strong with a steady kick, the current bearing him downstream.

Jack had Blackmon take him and Alligator over in the launch. He wore the Airlight .38 on his belt.

"She's not worth it," Blackmon said. "Best thing could happen would be Tudor finds her."

"Shut up," Jack said.

"Don't you hurt Tudor," Blackmon said. "He's a good Mississippi boy. Never done any harm to you."

"Him doing harm's what I'm worried about," Jack said.

They reached the bank, the driftwood log still floating in an eddy. Jack followed Tudor's tracks up the bank and into the tangle of cane, greenbriar, and grapevines.

Jack walked straight for the levee as he knew Tudor would have done. After a few hundred yards he hit a dirt track and followed it. In an hour he stood on the levee, looking down at the fields spread out before him. A herd of Brahman cattle with their humps and floppy ears grazed on the side of the levee. After pulling out his shirttails to conceal the pistol, he put Alligator back on his chain and walked down off the levee. He caught a ride with a farmer who dropped him off where the county road hit Highway 61.

At the crossroads was a small store just like the one in Egypt Ridge: tin roof, ancient gas pumps, and rusting cars in the side yard. A fat woman stood behind the cash register. Two lean men sat in broken-down easy chairs watching a football game on a black-and-white television set. One wore an Ole Miss baseball cap.

"Is that a mean dog?" the woman asked.

"Sure is," one of the men answered.

"Quiet," the other said. "The Rebels are getting ready to make a field goal."

"Mister, take that dog out of here," the woman said.

"You seen a girl with long blond hair?" Jack asked.

"She your wife?" the woman asked.

"No," Jack said.

"Took the bus this morning for New Orleans," the one with the cap said.

"Other feller her husband?" the woman asked.

"Who?" Jack asked.

"Little man with a shotgun," she said. "Smells like fish. Smells about as bad as that dog. He's asleep out back. Waiting for the next bus."

Jack walked past the TV set and out the back of the store. Under a black walnut tree, its leaves just starting to turn yellow around the edges, he found Tudor asleep. The shotgun leaned against the tree.

Tudor opened his eyes when Jack walked up. The people from the store were watching from the back steps.

"She deserves it," Tudor said.

Jack stepped over and took the shotgun. He worked the bolt, shucking the shells out on the ground. Then he fieldstripped the gun and put the bolt in his pocket. He gave the gun back to Tudor, who slung it over his shoulder.

"She sure skinned you," Tudor said. "I'll be back on the river, my chillen eating molasses and catfish. You won't be growing no cotton."

Jack walked off.

"Texas Firecracker's gonna kill that dog of yours!" Tudor yelled. "Dog that loses won't be worth nothing."

Jack went around the side of the store and out to the highway, where he caught a ride with a trucker headed for New Orleans. Alligator sat between them, panting from the heat, but the trucker never complained about the stink of the dog. He even petted him from time to time, and as always Alligator ignored him.

"Dog don't have much to say," the man said.

"He's a fighting dog, not a pet," Jack said.

Jack watched the fields pass by and thought that Tudor was right. Everything depended on Alligator now, forty pounds of bone and muscle that knew nothing except fighting, neither wanting nor needing kind words and petting.

He thought too of Amy, wondering if his pursuit of her was as foolish as Tudor had claimed. Now that he had stopped Tudor there was no reason to seek her out in New Orleans. But every time he let his mind wander, there she was: blond hair, emerald earrings flashing in the light, and he was drawn after her just as irresistibly as the brown river rolled between the tall green levees toward the blue Gulf.

Chapter Twenty-One

Jack got off the truck on Canal Street. He looked up Uncle Charles Musson's name in the directory, not expecting to find him still living in the city, but it was there. He called him from a phone booth. Uncle Charles did not seem happy to hear from him until Jack told him about the big fight between Alligator and the Texas Firecracker. And when Jack told his uncle he had Alligator with him, Charles gave him directions to his apartment in the French Quarter on Bienville Street.

He wandered down into the Quarter through the narrow streets, the apartments, bars, shops, and restaurants fronted with ancient bricks, black ironwork, and weathered wood painted in dark colors. Amy could be anywhere, probably already set up in business again. Everywhere there was a damp moldy smell as if the streets had been flooded, the water only recently receded. It was a hot day, as hot as July in Egypt Ridge although it was September, but the heat was different, heavier, the air thick and humid. His running shoes felt as if they were filling up with water, the city like a piece of melon lying rotting in the sun with flies swarming around it.

He thought of those football weekends he had spent in the city with his friends who had gone to Ole Miss to study to become doctors and lawyers and bankers. Everything would have been so much easier if he could have been like them. No Vietnam, no risking his neck growing the plants, and no Amy. By now he would be married to one of those pretty sorority girls and have a house in the suburbs of Memphis and a couple of kids.

Instead of a doctor's beeper, he wore the Airlight .38 on his belt.

He wanted to find Amy, but at the same time hoped he would not. There was sure to be a fight, and he was not sure he was going to be able to keep the gun in its holster.

Uncle Charles lived in a small upstairs apartment. He was a small, hawk-nosed man, dressed in a sleeveless T-shirt and a pair of cutoff jeans, who opened the door with a camera in his hand and started taking pictures of Alligator.

"He a crazy dog?" Charles asked.

"Sure is," Jack said.

"You watch him," Charles said.

But Charles ignored Alligator, squatting inches from his face as he took close-ups.

"Hasn't been fought much?" Charles said.

"Twice," Jack said. "Killed the dogs."

"Easy to tell," Charles said. "Not a mark on him."

Charles reached out and petted Alligator on the head.

"Careful," Jack said, putting his hand on Alligator to let him know it was all right.

"Don't worry," Charles said. "I know these dogs."

The walls were covered with pictures of dogs and fights. Jack recognized his father and Blackmon in some of the fight scenes. And in all the pictures of the dogs, whether fighting or posed for the artist, the same qualities of violence and death and evil came through. It was as if all the dogs had just scrambled up out of hell, what Jack feared most in Alligator repeated over and over in the pictures.

"Dexter carried me around to dogfights after he married Margaret," Charles said. "Pretty soon I'd stopped painting anything except dogs. Couldn't get those dogs out of my mind. Still can't."

Alligator lay down and went to sleep in front of the air conditioner.

"Woman lived with me for a few years," Charles continued. "Left. Couldn't stand having the pictures around. Said it was like trying to make love on top of one of the tombs in Saint Louis Cemetery."

Jack noticed some of the same gifts he had received from Margaret lined up on a shelf: a porcelain from West Germany, a Swiss music box, and a carved African mask.

"Margaret sent me a stuffed piranha," Charles said. "You know she took a boat up the Amazon. She send you a stuffed fish?"

"No, I got a machete," Jack said.

"Don't know how Dexter put up with her as long as he did," Charles said. "Sister always said she wouldn't be tied down to one man."

"Daddy fucked every woman in the Delta," Jack said.

"Got a good start on it," Charles said, and laughed. "Margaret been back to see you?"

"No," Jack said.

Jack picked up the carved African mask, the black wood carved into a grotesque face, all the features distorted.

"She's been through here four or five times," Charles said. "Sometimes comes in on the boat. Sometimes on the plane. We go out and have dinner at Antoine's or Brennan's."

Jack wondered if Charles was lying about his mother. After all, he was a dogfighting friend of Dexter's. Probably drunk half the time.

"She come to see you?" Charles asked.

"Wouldn't come within a hundred miles of Daddy," Jack said.

"That's true," Charles said. "You'd lived in Jackson then she'd have been up to see you. You could count on it."

Jack told Charles about Dexter's scheme to get their land back and how Alligator had won his fights. Charles got excited and took more pictures of Alligator.

"All I'm good at is painting fighting dogs," Charles said. "Nobody wants pictures of dogfights. So I paint tourist trash: Saint Louis Cathedral, the Cabildo, the goddamn river. Do portraits of tourists on Jackson Square."

Jack told Charles about Amy, but he had seen nobody like her around the square.

"Sooner or later she'll show up," Charles said.

Alligator got up and took a stroll about the apartment. Charles followed him with the camera.

"I'll shoot pictures of the fight," Charles said. "He's going to be my best picture. Have to finish painting the mural in the courthouse. Probably want to throw me in jail when I show up."

Every day Jack went with Charles to the square and sat in a lawn chair by the iron fence and waited for Amy to appear while Charles did sketches of tourists. At night he locked Alligator in Charles's spare bedroom and prowled the bars in search of her.

Weeks passed and Jack knew that he could not stay much longer. He had talked to Dexter on the phone and promised to bring Alligator home. Dexter was afraid the dog was going to lose his conditioning. Jack learned the riverboat had been boarded by the narcotics officers, who after finding nothing and questioning everyone had let them go.

Jack started taking Alligator for early-morning runs in Audubon Park. He was afraid to take the dog off the chain so together they jogged beneath the live oaks. Alligator was in good shape, but Jack knew he needed to get him home so he could seriously prepare for the fight, which was only a few weeks away. Dexter liked to remove a dog to a special holding pen a few days before a fight, away from all distractions.

"Dog knows a fight's coming," Dexter liked to say. "Needs to meditate on it. Like those Buddhists do."

Dexter would probably want to keep Alligator in the house. Jack had almost given up any hope of finding Amy, deciding that it was likely she had left the city or maybe even the country to escape the attention of the Mississippi narcotics officers.

One morning they ended their run by the gate to the zoo. Employees were coming in to work, some dressed in jumpsuits with the zoo logo on the shoulder. Alligator, who had been lying panting in the shade of a tree, suddenly got up, his ears raised, and watched one group going along the walk. Jack tugged on the chain and told the dog to sit down. Suddenly Alligator gave the chain a tug that almost pulled the nylon loop out of Jack's hands.

Then he saw her, dressed in a sundress, her blond hair pulled back in a long ponytail. He started toward her, the dog straining against the lead and making wheezing sounds as the collar cut off his breathing.

She heard the chain rattling and stopped. When she turned and saw them, she did not even seem surprised, just afraid of the dog, who had almost gotten out of control. Jack pulled him up short ten yards from her and made him stand at heel, which he did, but his whole body was quivering in anticipation of getting at her.

"Keep him away," she said.

Jack made Alligator sit and walked closer to her while still holding the lead.

"What are you going to do?" she asked.

"I want to talk to you," he said.

"I came to study the snakes," she said. "I don't have time for you."

He followed her into the zoo, and they walked to the reptile house.

"Only thing I ever learned of any use is what Dumas taught me about snakes," she said, looking through one of the viewing windows. "That's a Russell's viper."

"I can read the sign," he said.

Alligator knew the snakes were there on the other side of the windows. He sniffed the air, walking stiff legged, his whole body tense.

"I learned about that snake from the books I got at the library," she said. "I'm going to take biology and zoology courses at LSU. Maybe I'll go to graduate school. Specialize in herpetology. Get a job out here."

"Why, you couldn't study nursing without hooking on the side," Jack said. "You don't know anything about snakes. Learned a couple of new words and think you're an expert."

"Don't tell me what I know," she said. "You don't know anything about me. I'm going to get a job out here."

She tapped her fingers against the glass, but the snake, lying coiled on the gravel, did not respond.

Jack wished he were like Alligator, who only knew how to fight and thought of nothing else. Then this girl would not be making a fool of him.

"You have my heart," he said.

He felt as if he were caught in the river at flood while she watched impassively from the bank as the brown water swept him away.

She stepped close to him, reaching up for his chest with her fingers and tracing his scars with her fingertips through his still-wet T-shirt.

"You were always sweet to me," she said.

Alligator shook his head, rattling the chain.

"God, that dog stinks," she said. "He wants to bite my head off. You watch him."

"I'll take care of you. I won't let anything happen to you," Jack said.

She said, "I can take care of myself."

She turned away and watched a python climbing up a log.

"I can't go back to Egypt Ridge," she continued. "Can't even go back to Mississippi."

"I'll move down here," he said.

"No, go fight that dog," she said. "Get that precious land of yours back."

Jack realized she was serious about going back to school. What she had learned from Dumas might be valuable. Alligator stood on his hind legs and sniffed at the glass.

"That dog belongs in a cage," she said.

"I'll come down and see you after the fight," he said.

"I don't want to hear any more about dogfights," she said.

"Do you want me to come?" he asked.

Alligator tugged on the lead, sniffing another window.

"Get in there with that bushmaster and you'll be a dead dog," she said. "All that stuff Dumas fed you won't do any good."

Alligator stopped and looked at her. Jack stroked his head, worried that the dog's eyes would begin to glaze over and he would become unmanageable.

She smiled and said, "Baby, you can send your daddy down anytime."

Jack was glad he had left the Airlight .38 in Musson's apartment although breaking her neck would be a simple thing. But the thought of harming her frightened him. It was as if some of Alligator had become part of him, a kind of stink on his soul that would never leave him.

He walked out of the dark reptile house into the bright sunlight.

"I warned you about me," she called after him.

But there was a break in her voice, a timbre that made him want to turn around and walk back inside. Alligator tugged on the lead and he kept walking.

They went through the zoo gates, the green leaves of the live oaks shining in the sun. Alligator walked beside him, panting in the heat, carrying his tail high, his claws clicking on the sidewalk as he went along in that easy trot he could keep up for miles. One snap of those powerful jaws could sever the Firecracker's spine, leaving Dexter to peddle the dog's frozen sap to the highest bidders, and the thought of how much was riding on the dog, all seven hundred acres contained within that forty pounds, caused Jack to shudder just as he sometimes did at a woman's touch.

Chapter Twenty-Two

Dexter held a meeting to prepare for the fight, which was only a week away, the day after Halloween. Squirrel and Dumas and Evelyn were there along with Charles, now Dexter's houseguest, who had driven Jack home in his van. Charles spent his time taking pictures of Alligator and working on the mural at the courthouse. Jack expected the people of Egypt Ridge to complain about Amy, but no one said a word. Francis gave him free beer at the store, and the ladies baked him pies as if there had been a death in the family.

But not everyone took it so well. Tudor had come home, and after administering a beating to his pale, thin wife, he went off to poach deer on the island for sale in Memphis. Wade had locked himself in his office with a shotgun and a bottle of Jack Daniel's black label for an entire day. Everyone waited for the shot, wondering if he was planning to pull the trigger with his toe. Then one of the deputies reported there had been a knifing at a black nightclub in which a saxophone player in a blues band had been cut up by both of his girlfriends. Wade came out of the office with an empty bottle and sober. He loved blues music and never missed the chance to personally investigate a knifing. Norris went to bed and would not get up to come to work. After three days, Sally Ann scooped Norris Junior's sand bucket full of a fire ant mound, which she dumped on her sleeping husband. Norris still whined and complained about the bites he received and kept waking up at night screaming the ants were on him. He smelled of insecticide and everyone said their bedroom did too. Blackmon blamed the loss on Jack and said he was going to get even with the Purses in the dogpit. Robert Red went back to managing the Duck Club and talked about taking a job flying an emergency medical helicopter for a Memphis hospital. Bascomb held a prayer breakfast at which he claimed he was again the happiest person in Mississippi.

"Those not working the pit will wear dinner jackets," Dexter said. "Ladies will wear a dress and heels. Just like the old days."

"Blood and evening clothes," Jack said. "That's good."

"It was a gentleman's sport then," Dexter said. "Before the trash took it up."

"Nothing can make it a gentleman's sport," Jack said. "You and your friends can fool each other, but you can't fool me. Watching dogs chew on each other is what it's about."

Alligator rolled over, rubbing his back against the floor.

"What's got you worked up?" Dexter asked. "Pussy, that's what it is. Should've left Amy alone, kept your pants on."

Evelyn said, "Bascomb said it was an act of God. Preached a good sermon about it in church."

"You-all got caught with that stuff and he'd be preacher to murderers and thieves at Parchman," Dexter said.

Charles got down on his hands and knees next to Alligator and sniffed at him.

"Don't smell like any dog I've ever seen," Musson said.

"Careful," Jack said. "Don't get too close."

Alligator yawned and stretched.

"Like the graveyard," Charles said. "Corpse gas leaking out of a tomb. Light a match near it and it makes a little blue pop."

"Squirrel says you been feeding Alligator rattlesnake venom," Dexter said to Dumas. "That why that dog smells so bad?"

"And some other stuff," Squirrel said. "Organic compounds from plants. Lab couldn't identify them."

"What you been up to?" Dexter asked Dumas.

"Firecracker dog has got twenty pounds on Alligator," Dumas said. "I want Alligator to taste bad."

Alligator, who lay at Jack's feet, raised his head at the sound of the old man's voice.

"Blackmon'll find a way to cheat if he can," Jack said.

"I'm washing the Firecracker myself," Dexter said. "Blackmon won't be putting poison on him."

Jack was glad Dexter was going to do it. He hated washing an opponent's dog. The one time he had done it he felt as if the dog's smooth belly skin were going to dissolve under his hands, spilling the steaming guts out onto the floor.

Dumas chuckled and said, "What we've got is on the inside."

"Won't make any difference," Squirrel said.

"How you know what those dogs can taste or smell?" Dumas asked.

Dexter said, "I want you to stop." He turned to Jack. "I want him on the catmill every day. Run that poison out of him."

Instead of taking more pictures of Alligator, Charles shot a roll of film on Evelyn. He had paid plenty of attention to her, making Dexter mad.

"I'll make you a print of the best one," Musson said. "Maybe I'll paint a picture from it."

"Stick to dogs, Charlie," Dexter said. "You're no good at painting women."

Evelyn got up and went out of the house. Musson followed her, ignoring the mean look Dexter gave him when he did.

"Why that damn Cajun is old enough to be her grandfather," Dexter said. "Charlie dresses like a hippie. Sleeping in my house, eating my food, and trying to move in on her."

Jack enjoyed watching Dexter uneasy.

"Maybe they're just good friends," Jack said. "And if they're not, he's probably too old to get it up anymore."

"Boy, don't you start fucking with me," Dexter said. "Remember, when I buy back our place you'll be working for me."

Dexter took Alligator's lead and went out into the backyard with the dog.

"Leave him alone," Squirrel said. "He's counting on this fight."

"So am I," Jack said.

They had come so close with the plants, the land slipping away from him like August dust through his fingers.

At the end of the fight, Alligator was not going to be lying dead on the bloody floor of the pit. Somehow he would beat the Firecracker, beat him even if the dog was fanged and clawed like a lion because Alligator could do nothing but fight and knew no fear.

Jack went every day to watch Charles work on the mural at the courthouse, the chewing tobacco and cigarette smell replaced by that of fresh paint. Evelyn was always there. She helped Musson mix his paints and brought him lunches. She was still mad at Dexter.

He enjoyed watching Dexter eat breakfast with Charles every morning. Dexter tried to insult him, but Musson paid no attention to him. The artist's manners were flawless. He could butter a biscuit with a grace that was maddening to Dexter, never dropping a crumb. Some mornings he expected Dexter to reach across the table and strangle him on the spot. Musson was always bright and full of talk, excited about the work he was going to do that day. That made Dexter even madder.

Charles was working on a figure of a priest. Evelyn sat in a lawn chair watching and Jack stood with his back to the wall, Alligator at his feet. Dexter came down the hall, his tennis shoes squeaking on the marble floor.

"I want that dog kept up, away from people," Dexter said.

"Dumas says—," Jack began.

"It's what I say," Dexter said. "You had your chance growing those plants. But you blew it. Let that little hooker make fools of all of you."

"It wasn't Jack's fault," Evelyn said. "We've heard enough about that."

Alligator stretched his front and rear legs out to rest his belly against the cool marble floor.

"You had your chance too," Dexter said. "You threw in with 'em."

"What's the matter with you?" Evelyn asked.

"Nothing," Dexter said. "Don't want my silly-ass son to screw up this dogfight."

Charles was still working hard on the mural, as if he were not even aware they were there.

"Why, Dexter, I believe you're jealous," Evelyn said.

Dexter took her arm and pulled her down the hallway, away from Musson. Jack sat still and listened.

"You tell me what's going on," Dexter whispered. "You've never cared for painting before."

"I'll do what I want," Evelyn said. "I like Charles. I've never known anybody like him before. He's going to teach me how to draw."

"He's crazy. He'll paint priests one day and monster dogs the next."

Jack hoped he was going to get to watch Evelyn tell Dexter she hated him, that she was in love with Uncle Charles.

Evelyn said, "Nothing's changed between us."

"You sure?" Dexter asked.

"Don't crowd me," she said.

Dexter turned to Jack and said, "Bring that dog on home. Needs to get his mind set on the fight."

Dexter walked off.

"I think Dexter is jealous," Evelyn said.

She was smiling as if she had just been told she was going to get her land back.

"Probably already got a new girlfriend," Jack said.

"Hush up," Evelyn said. "Lived with him all these years and don't know a thing about him."

She walked off to help Musson mix his paints, leaving Jack alone with Alligator, who had gone to sleep on the floor.

* * *

Jack ran Alligator on the catmill early in the morning, the fight only one day away. People had come in for the fight from Texas and Louisiana, even from as far away as California. Dumas sat under an umbrella at the road to keep anyone from coming up to the house to get a look at Alligator. The dog pursued the fanged goblin mask around and around. Dexter had come out of the house to watch while Evelyn cooked breakfast. Musson was still asleep, having stayed up most of the night working on the mural.

"Remember he's fighting tomorrow," Dexter said.

"Dumas says a short workout won't hurt," Jack said.

"When you finish, I want you to put him in the house," Dexter said. "Next new thing he sees I want to be that Firecracker dog."

Alligator stopped and Jack took him out of the harness.

"I've always been afraid of that dog," Dexter said. "You afraid of him?"

"I'm smart so I'm afraid," Jack said.

"He likes you," Dexter said.

"Likes killing," Jack said.

Jack's scars itched, but he kept himself from reaching up to rub them in front of Dexter. He wondered if the Firecracker dog was going to be able to taste or smell the venom just as Dumas claimed.

"He'll fight for you," Dexter said.

"Maybe you should handle him," Jack said.

"See that?" Dexter said, pointing off across the fields toward the green hump of the Indian mound. "That dog's going to get that back for us. I want you in the pit with him."

"Won't be my fault if he gets beat," Jack said. "Dumas says he can't give up twenty pounds and win."

"Let me worry about that," Dexter said. "Next spring we'll be working that land."

Alligator tugged on the lead, looking out across the fields.

"Smells a rabbit," Dexter said. "That's why he needs to go inside until the fight. Wasting energy worrying about rabbits."

Evelyn called them to breakfast. Dumas came in from the road.

"What do you think that Firecracker dog will do?" Dexter asked Dumas.

"He's a leg dog," Dumas said. "Go for Alligator's back legs. But Alligator'll be too quick for him."

"Too big for Alligator to throw," Dexter said.

"Maybe he'll go for a chest hold," Dumas said. "Big dog won't be able to breathe right. Then it'll be over."

Charles came in to breakfast, wearing jeans and an unbuttoned shirt, the tails hanging out of his pants.

"How about a drink?" Dexter said.

"No drinking until I finish the mural," Charles said.

Evelyn glared at Dexter and poured Musson a cup of coffee.

"It's evening clothes tomorrow," Dexter said. "You need to go to Greenville to buy an outfit?"

"Got one in the car," Musson said.

Evelyn laughed. Dexter heaped jam on a piece of toast and ate it as if he were Alligator taking a bite out of an opponent.

They finished breakfast and Musson went off to work at the courthouse. Dumas returned to his post on the road. Jack lingered at the table, hoping to watch Evelyn and Dexter fight.

"The fight's tomorrow night, not now," Dexter said. "Go baby-sit that dog."

As he walked off, he heard Evelyn start in on Dexter about being jealous of Musson and what a good artist he was and how Dexter should be honored to have him stay at his house.

Jack went to his room and found Alligator asleep on the rug by his bed. He lay on the bed and stared up at the ceiling, smelling the stink of the dog and through the open window the early-autumn scent of barren fields and dead poplar leaves lying in heaps beneath the big tree by his window. A hawk hung in the high blue sky, turning in slow circles over the ditches and swamps.

How was the dog going to do in the fight? One mistake on Alligator's part and the larger dog would prevail. But Alligator had good moves and a strong bite and what was more important—he was game. Jack closed his eyes and for an instant Amy was there, her body soft beneath his hands. Then like a cloud across that pale autumn sun Alligator took her place: eyes glazed over with that milky film, muscles in his hind legs knotted and quivering, head twisting as he searched for where the big red dog lived.

Chapter Twenty-Three

On Saturday night the people who were going to attend the fight met in the gravel parking lot of Bascomb's church, the moonlight shining off the tin roof, the barren fields stretching away to distant lights. There Travis had provided a school bus driven by Wade to carry them to the fight. Once a person got on the bus, they could not get off or leave the fight until it was over.

They loaded the bus. Sally Ann snagged her evening gown on the door and got mad at Norris. Evelyn had refused to come, saying she could not bear to watch a dogfight. Jack found it strange watching the bus roll away from the church with the men in dinner jackets and the women in evening clothes as if it were a wedding party bound for a reception.

Jack followed in the truck with Dexter and Alligator. He felt the lump of the Airlight .38 under his jacket. Dexter was carrying ten thousand dollars to bet on the fight and had insisted Jack go armed. The old man was carrying a .44-caliber derringer that had belonged to his father.

Travis had arranged for them to use the gymnasium of the school. Now that the plants had failed the whole community turned their attention to the dogfight. Francis took bets in his store and kept odds, which were running three to one against Alligator. It was as if winning anything on the fight, even a small sum, would somehow make up for the loss of the crop. And some had borrowed money on their cars and homes and wagered much more than they could afford to lose.

The gym still had the Halloween decorations from the carnival the night before. The dunking machine had been pushed over into one corner, and a cardboard witch rode her broomstick on one wall. The school's red-eyed black panther mascot, crouched and ready to spring with bared teeth, was painted below the basketball scoreboard.

Jack and Dexter and Dumas had built the pit close to one of the rows of bleachers. It had plywood sides and a floor of green outdoor carpet. Dexter had taped scratch lines four feet out from each corner, the lines the dogs had to cross on a signal after their handlers had separated them. Any dog that shied away was declared the loser of the fight. Dexter told tales of dogs with broken forelegs who pushed themselves across the scratch line after their handlers had released them. Wash and rinse tubs full of warm water had been placed behind each corner so the dogs could be washed before the fight. A double set of tubs avoided the necessity of a coin toss to see which dog would be washed first. The first dog would have to wait for the second dog to be washed and that meant using up energy he would need later in the pit.

They took Alligator out of the truck, the dog standing on the gravel like an iron statue, turning his head slowly and sniffing the air to locate his enemy.

"Knows he's getting ready to fight," Dexter said. "Put the muzzle on him. Already going crazy." He turned to Jack. "You mind him. I'm counting on you."

Jack slipped the muzzle on the dog, talking softly to him, but it all did no good. The dog knew. And instead of the anticipation of a dogfight, Jack felt as he had before football games. There was that dry smell of dying grass, the crickets chirping with a slower beat, and the night was cool.

Inside people were standing about on the gym floor where the night before the blacks and the catfishermen had held their Halloween carnival. The smell of whiskey was in the air. Dumas and Dexter held leads attached to Alligator's collar. They tugged gently at the leads, afraid of doing anything to set him off, and guided the dog into the gym.

The crowd fell silent as they went across the floor, Alligator straining at the leads. Jack bent down and petted him, and it was like stroking a piece of iron, the dog rigid beneath his touch. The dog's claws clicked on the floor, his paws slipping as he attempted to gain purchase on the waxed surface.

Blackmon and the Texas Firecracker, a big red dog, waited by the side of the pit. The Firecracker was unmuzzled and Tudor knelt beside him, the lead wrapped around his hands. Alligator pretended not to even see the other dog, but it was all Dumas and Dexter could do to keep Alligator from pulling them over to Blackmon's corner. The Firecracker watched Alligator carefully but did not move. Jack picked up Alligator and carried him to prevent the dog from wasting any more precious energy.

"My chillen will get their diploma right here," Tudor said to Jack. "Won't be going to the private school."

"Alligator is gonna give the Firecracker his lesson tonight," Dexter said.

A Texas man, wearing a white cowboy hat with his tux, had been chosen as referee, and he directed them to wash their dogs. He issued them two towels apiece and a blanket. Dexter washed the Firecracker and Blackmon washed Alligator. Dexter took a long time doing the job and Blackmon complained.

"They're messing with my dog, Mr. Referee," he said. "Trying to get him worked up so he'll wear himself out before the fight starts."

The referee asked Dexter to hurry up.

Tudor dried Alligator with a towel and took him out of the tub. Alligator shook himself. Tudor started to wrap him in the blanket.

"Taste him," Blackmon said.

"No, that's not in the rules," Jack said.

"Was once," Blackmon said.

Dumas walked over from their corner.

"You washed him," Dumas said. "That's enough."

"What does the owner say?" Blackmon asked. "You have this old man taste the Firecracker."

"Go ahead," Dexter said. "We got nothing to hide."

So as dog men had done at the start of the sport in England, Tudor licked Alligator from head to tail, concentrating on his ears, nose, and hind legs.

"Don't taste nothing but soap," Tudor said. "But he smells like a skunk. Not fair for Firecracker to fight a dog that smells that bad."

"Take a bite," Dexter said. "He won't mind."

"Firecracker'll do all the biting," Tudor said.

Tudor wrapped Alligator in the blanket, and Jack picked him up. Alligator's stink had been brought out by the water. Squirrel was on the outside of the pit with a case of veterinary supplies. People were making bets in the crowd.

"One thousand on the black dog," a man shouted.

"You're covered," Francis said. He looked up into the crowd, holding his arms above his head, and yelled, "Anybody else?"

More bets were placed. Then Jack stopped listening and concentrated on Alligator. Dumas climbed out of the pit, leaving Jack alone with the dog still wrapped in the blanket and faced to the wall. He took Alligator's muzzle off and removed the blanket, feeling the dog begin to tremble beneath his hands. Jack felt sick, knowing the bond between himself and the dog, along with blood, was getting ready to drive Alligator into battle. And touching that wild, dark mystery that made Alligator fight made him afraid.

"Face your dogs, gentlemen," the referee said.

Jack wrapped both his arms around Alligator and waited for the referee's signal. He had already introduced the dogs and their owners, giving a summary of the animals' bloodlines.

"Ready, gentlemen," the referee said, nodding to the timekeeper, a man from Alabama, to write down the time. "Release your dogs."

The dogs ran straight for each other, meeting in the center of the pit.

The Firecracker tried for a leg hold, submarining under Alligator as he went for it, but Alligator threw his own hind leg up on his back, and the red dog's teeth snapped at air. The crowd gasped in approval. But immediately, as if at a signal, the crowd grew quiet, and the dogs fought in silence. Jack watched the muscles in Alligator's hind legs swell, and heard the tendons make little popping sounds as both dogs stood on their hind legs and used their front paws like a pair of wrestlers.

Jack went down on his hands and knees next to Alligator, encouraging the dog. Tudor's teeth were bared and the spit flew from his mouth as he talked to the Firecracker. Jack kept one eye on the little swamper in case he should come at him.

"Come on, baby," Jack said.

"Do it to him, Firecracker," Tudor urged.

The red dog got a hold on Alligator's shoulder and pushed him to the carpet, shaking him hard. Finally the red dog tired and paused. Alligator broke free and got a nose hold on the red dog, twisting and shaking his head to try to bring the dog to the carpet. But the red dog was too big and strong and broke the hold.

Fifteen minutes had gone by, and both dogs paused for a moment, standing inches away from each other. The red dog turned his head and shoulders away from Alligator and then went for an ear hold and shook Alligator.

"There's a turn!" Dumas shouted.

The referee allowed them to pick their dogs up because the red dog had turned away from Alligator. But it was another ten minutes before the red dog lost his hold and the dogs were separated. Jack ran across the pit and picked up Alligator, bringing him to the corner and turning his head to the wall. The referee tossed Dumas and Tudor a sponge. Now the red dog would have to scratch, to see if he was willing to cross the scratch line when released from his corner. Dumas worked on Alligator, wiping the blood off his shoulder. He checked his mouth for broken teeth and massaged him.

"See, he didn't keep hold long," Dumas whispered to Jack.

"Don't like the taste of him. Firecracker'll wear himself out. Then Alligator'll take over."

Jack wrapped his arms around Alligator, thinking of the dog's frozen sap and all the dogs it had the potential of making. He wished he were not there but at the same time had grown excited about the match. It looked as if Alligator had a chance of winning. The red dog did not seem to have his heart in the fight. The crowd was yelling, and he heard the voice of Francis as he took more bets.

"Get ready," the timekeeper called.

"Twenty-five seconds, gentlemen," the referee said. "Face your dogs."

Jack held Alligator, waiting for the charge of the Firecracker.

"Red dog ready?" the referee said.

Tudor nodded.

"Go," the timekeeper yelled.

"Release your dogs," the referee said.

Tudor released Firecracker, the dog shooting across the pit with no hesitation. Jack waited until he was only a few feet away and then released Alligator. Alligator submarined under the red dog, twisting his head and going for a hold on a hind leg. But he missed and then the red dog closed his jaws on Alligator's hind leg. Jack did not hear bone cracking, the red dog's teeth going straight through just above the hock. Alligator got a hold on the red dog's shoulder, both dogs now locked together, each shaking the other, until they both were exhausted and paused. The fight was now an hour and a half old.

"Crunch that bone," Tudor said to Firecracker. "Want to hear it break."

"He's running out of gas," Jack said to Alligator. "Hang on."

"Red dog'll let go," Dumas kept saying. And then in a whisper when Jack came close to the corner, "Won't like the taste."

Fifteen minutes passed, both dogs still locked together, and each occasionally shaking his hold. Jack did not believe the Firecracker was going to let go any time soon, and when he did Alligator would be doomed by an injured hind leg, at the mercy of the larger dog. But then the red dog relaxed his hold, allowing Alligator to twist free.

"That old man's putting poison on him," Tudor yelled at the referee. "You watch him."

The crowd cheered and more money passed hands. The red dog turned again when Alligator went for a hold on his upper jaw. Jack picked Alligator up at the next opportunity. He sponged him off, Tudor yelling all the time to the referee to watch to look out for poison. Jack massaged Alligator while Dumas checked his hind leg. The fight was now almost two hours old.

"Went clean through," Dumas said. "Bones all right."

"You watch that old man, Mr. Referee," Tudor shouted. "I want to taste their water."

And leaving his cousin to work on the Firecracker, Tudor came across the pit.

"Go ahead," Dexter said.

Dumas handed him the pail, and Tudor scooped up some in his palm and drank.

"Drink the whole damn pail," Jack said.

Tudor spit out the water.

"Tastes of blood. That's all," Tudor yelled across the pit to Blackmon.

Dumas worked on the leg until the referee ordered them to face their dogs. Firecracker hesitated just for a moment before he ran across the pit at Alligator, and the dogs went at it again, both animals covered with blood and the carpet wet and slick with it. By now the crowd had become sluggish just like the dogs, but fortified by whiskey they still urged their favorites on.

Alligator's left ear had been shredded and a stream of blood ran down his left hind leg, but he continued to fight, never giving the slightest hint he was considering turning away from the red dog. The red dog scratched three more times, each time hesitating more than the last before he shot across the pit toward Alligator's corner. Tudor kept complaining to the referee that Dumas was putting poison on Alligator.

As the fight came up on the three-hour mark, both dogs were fighting in slow motion. Firecracker got Alligator down by using his superior weight and bit deep into his shoulder again, shaking him as a terrier would shake a rat until, exhausted, the red dog collapsed on top of him.

"Kill him, kill him," Tudor chanted.

"Get up, baby," Jack coaxed, his face not six inches away from Alligator's head.

He smelled the sweet scent of blood.

"Got that red dog now," Dumas shouted. "Worn out."

But Alligator did not look much better to Jack. The dog should be lying in some quiet place with a quart of Ringer's solution draining into him.

Jack took one step to pick up Alligator but suddenly the dog twisted beneath the big red dog and found a chest hold, rolling the Firecracker dog over at the same time and shaking the larger dog. The red dog wheezed and coughed as he tried to breathe. Then the Firecracker quit fighting.

"That's it," Blackmon said. "You win."

"Alligator of Top Dog Kennels wins in three hours and ten minutes," the referee announced.

Sally Ann began to yell at Norris for betting on the wrong dog.

"Damn dog bit my finger off," Norris complained. "Can't bet on him."

Norris wiggled his finger, now good as new except for the scar, in Sally Ann's face.

But Wade and Robert Red and Francis were winners.

"My own club," Robert Red shouted as he collected money from the losers in the crowd, who moaned and cursed.

Jack took the breaking stick and stepped forward, but Dexter snatched it from him.

"It's not over yet," Dexter said. "Goddamn, he's dead game. Can't beat that big dog. He'll fight to the death, keep fighting as he dies. You'll see."

Dexter knelt beside Alligator and inserted the tip of the stick in the back of his jaw.

"Pick up your dog, Blackmon," Dexter said. "Alligator'll fight until he's dead. You'll see."

"They fight anymore and both those dogs are going to die," Blackmon said. "My dog's done with fighting today."

"They put poison on that little dog," Tudor said.

"Shut up," Blackmon said. "It was a fair fight. You won."

Tudor ran over and tasted Alligator's water again.

"Nothing, goddammit," Tudor said.

Dexter looked toward the crowd and said, "He'd be dead game. Damn red dog quit."

Jack realized Dexter had counted on the Firecracker dog beating Alligator. Alligator was supposed to die still fighting, and that would make him worth at least double the value at stud among men who spoke the words "dead game" to one another as if it were some sort of incantation or holy password.

Dexter twisted the stick to try and make Alligator let go. Musson stepped into the pit and rapidly shot one picture after another with his camera.

"Pinch his nostrils shut," Blackmon suggested.

Dexter put his hand on Alligator's nose. Suddenly the dog let go and turned on Dexter, knocking him to the carpet. Alligator twisted his head to find a hold beneath the old man's ribs and began to shake, it all happening so fast that no one had a chance to move. It seemed to Jack to take him forever to take the three steps to his father and pull the Airlight .38 out of its holster.

He put the barrel in Alligator's ear, inclining it parallel to Dexter's chest, and pulled the trigger. Instead of releasing the hold, Alligator shook the old man harder. Jack pulled the trigger again. Alligator kept shaking. After the third round, he was still, but they had to use the breaking stick to pry his jaws apart.

"Goddamn, that dog is sure enough dead game," someone in the crowd yelled.

Dexter looked bad. He had turned the grey color of November

soybean stubble and was barely conscious. Squirrel shot the Ringer's solution he had brought for Alligator into his arm and they carried him to Musson's van for transport to the hospital.

Jack rode with him, Dexter stretched out on the metal floor amid the cans of paint and half-finished pictures of pit bulls in action. He did not want Dexter to die. He had wished him dead a thousand times, but now his father looked frail and old as if in one bite Alligator had robbed him of what little was left of his youth.

"Hurry!" Jack yelled to Musson. "Hurry."

Chapter Twenty-Four

Dexter escaped with just two broken ribs from his encounter with Alligator. He had bet for Alligator to lose and the ten thousand was gone. But people had heard about the semen stored under liquid nitrogen, and the phone rang constantly with inquiries from breeders. Dexter talked to them, quoting prices and writing down orders in an account book. Musson had gone back to New Orleans, saying he was going to paint his masterpiece, a huge canvas of Alligator's attack on Dexter. Evelyn had practically moved in. She kept saying it was just for a few days, until Dexter was better. Jack liked having her in the house.

He had been worried about his father, but now the old man was better, except for some sore ribs. He realized they were both being wary of each other, afraid of doing or saying something to start the battle between them again. Jack knew one day the fight would resume. He had promised himself not to let himself forget what the old man had done to his mother. But Dexter was not back to his old self.

Jack found Dexter on the back porch one afternoon standing in front of the liquid-nitrogen refrigerator and regarding it as if he were a demolition man getting ready to defuse an artillery shell.

"When you going to start selling?" Jack asked.

"When I'm ready," Dexter said.

Jack left his father alone, going out in the backyard and looking at the bare fields that by spring could be theirs again.

*   *   *

Evelyn had just served them a big breakfast, but Dexter had eaten almost nothing.

"Biscuits too done?" Evelyn asked.

"Fine," Dexter said. "Just not hungry."

Dexter went out onto the back porch. Jack started to follow, but Evelyn took him by the arm and kept him in the kitchen.

"Leave him alone," she said.

Later Jack was sitting on the front porch when Dexter appeared carrying a military ammo box he used to carry shotgun shells on dove hunts.

"Let's go for a ride," said Dexter, who wore one of Evelyn's pistols at his hip.

"We going shooting?" Jack asked.

"Boy, you ask too damn many questions," Dexter said.

Dexter drove out across the levee and then to Margaret's park. The roof of the arbor had fallen in, and honeysuckle vines had climbed up the sides. A jungle of weeds and small trees had grown up, much of it sumac whose leaves had turned blood red. Jack followed Dexter, who carried the ammo box, into the jungle, and they made their way to the sandbar. Jack kept expecting to step on a snake but gave up worrying about it because he seldom could even see his own feet in the tangle.

They came out of the jungle onto the sandbar, the river wide and brown before them, the Arkansas shore thick with willows whose leaves had mostly fallen off, leaving the bare trunks growing at an angle over the water. Dexter walked down to the water, the river making a sucking sound as it moved past the sandbar. He put the ammo box on the sand.

"Margaret loved this place," Dexter said.

Jack wished he had left Alligator alone. A few more seconds and the dog might have killed the old man.

"Too bad you didn't love her," Jack said.

"For once be still and listen," Dexter said. "I've had my share of women. But she was the one who started it. Couldn't leave any man alone. Finally fell in love with one. Owned a big wholesale grocery company in Memphis. Told that grocery man she was going to marry him. Next thing I know, she left him and me and you and went off to Peru to see some deserted city. Why would a woman run off to Peru? I could understand her going to New York or Paris but not to some stone city up in the mountains. And by herself. She went by herself."

"Goddamn lie," Jack said.

"Evelyn knows. Everyone knows," Dexter said. "Ask anyone. Knew how you felt about Margaret so they kept it from you."

Jack wished the river would rise and sweep away both him and Dexter along with what was left of the park.

"I loved her too," Dexter said. "Still do."

"All those women?" Jack said.

"Didn't love them," Dexter said. "Loved her. She knew it. Didn't care what I did."

Jack felt as if he had stepped into a quicksand pool in one of the swamps, the sand sucking him down, filling his lungs with a wet, scratchy thickness as he tried to breathe.

"You can hate me or love me," Dexter said. "Should've told you the truth that day in Greenville when you sneaked into the house and spied on me."

Jack tried to picture his mother climbing a jungle-covered mountain to a deserted stone city. Dexter had driven her away.

"Right now I want to kill you," Jack said.

"Can't believe any son of mine would be such a damn fool," Dexter said. "Why didn't you let the dog do it then?"

Dexter took the pistol out of the holster, Evelyn's favorite .357, and offered it butt first to Jack.

"Go ahead," Dexter said. "Killing's easy. Living's hard. Thought you'd learned that in the war."

Jack took the pistol. His scars itched, and he scratched at them with his free hand.

"What are you waiting for?" Dexter asked. "Thought you

wanted me dead. I'm not going to do it myself. You'll have to take your chances with the law."

The pistol in his hand felt as if it weighed a thousand pounds, his arm hanging slack by his side.

Dexter took hold of his arms just above the elbow, the grip still strong and firm as Jack tried to pull away.

"I love you," Dexter said.

"Love nothing but killing," Jack said.

Dexter knelt down and opened the ammo box, the lid popping open with a clank. He pulled out a handful of the plastic straws.

"Can't let people breed more crazy dogs," Dexter said.

"You're crazy!" Jack said. "They're already ruined."

Jack tossed the pistol on the sand and took a straw out of the box. Holding it up to the light he saw the crystals were gone. Nothing remaining but a milkshake slush. Now he felt like shooting Dexter and was glad he had dropped the pistol.

"Like selling little pieces of hell," Dexter said. "Some of Alligator's rubbed off on you. Better watch out. Look what's happened to Charlie. Down in New Orleans painting pictures nobody wants to buy. Scare the hell out of them if they did."

"The land?" Jack said.

"Lost," Dexter said.

Dexter began to toss the straws into the river one by one. They floated on the brown water, bobbing in the current.

Dexter said, "For the fish."

"How will you live?" Jack asked.

Dexter picked up the ammo box and emptied the rest of the straws into the river.

"Best way I can. Same way you will," Dexter said. "You want that land bad enough you'll get it back. Same way your Grandfather Purse got it in the first place. Scratched and clawed and fought for it. Survived yellow fever and floods and reconstruction. Still got the island. Guess we could be hunting and fishing guides for a while. What do you say?"

Jack embraced his father, hugging him as tight as he had held Alligator in the pit.

"Careful. My ribs," Dexter said.

A towboat pushing a string of barges came into view around the bend and gave a blast on its horn.

"Maybe I can find some work in New Orleans," Jack said. "Offshore oil. That's good money."

"Go down there if you want," Dexter said.

"I could get with Amy again," Jack said.

Dexter said, "She down there? Be careful. She's trouble."

"My trouble," Jack said.

Jack measured himself against the old man, waiting for him to make a move. Instead Dexter turned and looked out at the river.

"Never will learn about women," Dexter said, speaking the words to the river.

The straws were gone now, floating down to the Gulf, and there was just the empty brown water and the towboat approaching in the distance. It blew its horn again. Dexter looked old and frail.

They left the sandbar. Dexter had trouble climbing up the slope into the jungle, and Jack gave him his hand, pulling him up the slippery bank. He led Dexter into the dense insect-loud tangle of cane, briars, and sumac, holding branches aside and breaking trail as together they walked across the ruined park to the truck.

About the Author

SCOTT ELY, a native of Atlanta, Georgia, received an M.A. from the University of Mississippi and an M.F.A. from the University of Arkansas. A Vietnam veteran, he is the author of *Starlight*, a critically acclaimed novel about Vietnam. Mr. Ely lives in South Carolina, where he teaches.